SPRING FEVER

J L ROBINSON

For my family.

CONTENTS

1
THE PARISH COUNCIL MEETING

Stephanie walked over to the patio door and sipped her tea. She never tired of looking out across the peaceful field, an ever-changing view according to the seasons. Now it was early Spring, the field was covered in grass and still had the straw like remains of the maize that had grown the previous year. The Proctor's farm grew different crops there, her favourite was wheat as she loved the way it rustled and swayed in the breeze. This morning, windswept birds struggled to fly across the troubled, grey sky overhead. No sign of any rabbits- they were sensibly snuggled together in their warm beds she imagined, where she wished she was right now.

Realising the time, Stephanie motivated

herself to think about work. Should she take the car even though the village school was only 5 minutes away or should she brave the weather and walk? It didn't look that bad outside.

"Walk it is," she decided.

She walked through the tidy kitchen into the utility room, grabbed her coat and scarf and walked back into the open plan dining area. She picked up her laptop bag, quickly strode across the living room and out the front door.

"Well, I'm wide awake now," she grimaced.

Her hair was blowing across her face as she battled to put the key in the lock, then she purposefully strode down the road to school.

#

The day had flown by as it usually did, never a dull day working with children. Stephanie's friend since school, Lisa, had worked with her as a teaching assistant for 5 years now so they were strong friends as well as work colleagues. Lisa tidied the side of the classroom while Stephanie finished marking the maths books, setting some aside to work with a group the next day.

"Right, I'll be going then," Lisa said as she reached for her coat. "I'll see you at the Village Hall tonight then?"

"Oh, I'd forgotten about the Council

meeting," Stephanie admitted.

"You are going, aren't you? I'm not going if you're not!"

"I suppose so…" Stephanie laughed, "do you fancy going for a drink at the pub after?"

"Yeah, I'll check with Martin and the kids, but it'll be fine."

"At least you've got a husband to check with," Stephanie sighed.

"Oh no you don't! "Lisa warned. "Young, free and single-I'm the one who's jealous! Hey, you'll never guess who Martin saw at the pub last night…. Mark Proctor. Blast from the past-Mr tall, dark and handsome himself."

Stephanie felt herself redden, "I wonder what he's doing back?"

Lisa shrugged, "I bet a few people will be surprised to see him, he hasn't been around since he moved to London."

"At least he's done something with his life! I bet it's exciting living in London, no wonder he hasn't been back."

"I wonder if we'll see anything of him. Didn't you have a thing for him at school?" Lisa teased.

"Well didn't everyone? Goodbye Lisa!"

Stephanie widened her eyes as a warning and started tidying her desk.

"See you at 7." she smiled.

Stephanie couldn't help but feel excited at the prospect of seeing Mark again. He was in the year above her at school and always had adoring girls surrounding him. Of course, she always felt tongue tied whenever their paths crossed, which really annoyed her. In fact, she hated to admit that she used to have a huge crush on him. Then he moved on, and Stephanie went on to train at teaching college in Lincoln.

"Maybe I should be more adventurous," she told herself.

She pulled herself together. "Well, it's good to be near my parents and I do love this village. I love the countryside and wouldn't last long in a big city anyway."

#

The walk home was less windy.

"Bye Miss!" a small group of children shouted across the road. Stephanie smiled and waved warmly. She turned the corner, past a small old farm with ducks and geese pecking at the soil. She watched through the wire fence and noticed work men had started to clear land further back to build new houses. No doubt that will be on the agenda at tonight's meeting. Everyone had been discussing it on social media and most people in the village were worried about what this would mean for the village.

It would be a shame for the place to grow, she mused as she walked along past the church. She liked the fact that in the Spring, ducks waddled about the streets with their ducklings running behind them. She loved that cars had to drive slowly in case a peacock decided to cross the road. There was a small family of peacocks that had escaped from the farm and now seemed to wander about as if they owned the place, often roosting on garage roofs crying out eerily to each other.

Opposite the church, was another area of land that had been cleared for a housing development. Stephanie had often imagined building a lovely big house there, with a pool house at the end of the garden overlooked by the magnificent weeping willow tree. It must have been growing there for years. She hoped they would keep it.

By now Stephanie had reached the end of her road. She passed the small play area where some boys were playing football. On the left was a stream that flowed between her house and the fields at the back. Stephanie liked having a stream at the end of her garden. It meant there were always ducks splashing about and even a pair of kingfishers faithfully returned year after year to nest in the bank. Yep, she couldn't think of living anywhere else. Not yet anyway.

#

After a quick bite, it was soon time for Stephanie to set off for the Parish Council meeting. The village hall was on the top road which led to the nearest town of Rigby. It was quite a modern building, considering that Hibaldton dated back hundreds of years. In fact, the village was built on an old roman road. The village hall was on one level, with windows overlooking the road on one side, and the playing fields on the other. It had a decent local cricket team and football team. A skateboard ramp was a new addition to the play area however the tennis court had got shabby.

As Stephanie walked along the road, she remembered when she and Lisa had decided to dig out their old rackets last summer inspired by Wimbledon, only to find the surface was so crumbled that the ball never bounced straight. Stephanie crossed the road into the car park which already was full of cars, she could see Lisa's short black hair sticking out of her bobble hat and her face beamed at Stephanie,

"Hurray, you made it then."

"How could I miss the opportunity to sit and

listen to Bryan Grayling MP making all the important decisions for us. I don't know what we'd do without him."

"Shh he'll hear us," Lisa giggled as they entered the building.

#

"EH ERM! Can I have everyone's attention and we'll start the meeting," Mr Grayling raised his voice above the chatter.

Around the wide, dark wooden table, sat the Parish Council. It had been a good turnout, Stephanie noticed. Mr Grayling, the council chairman sat at the head of the table. He was maybe in his mid-sixties, glasses and a balding head on the top with short brown hair at the sides. He always wore a suit and tie and lived in an ostentatious house, The Old Vicarage. Through the window, Stephanie could see the roof of his house from where she sat.

Behind the chairman, on the wall, was a long-framed map of the village. It was quite a recent map which showed the fields, farms and houses with the names of the streets winding in between. Stephanie thought this room was very old fashioned and posh for a village hall. The table looked like it belonged in a Town Hall and the chair, at the head of the table, was larger and ornate with dark arms curling at the ends. Bryan Grayling sat there like a king surveying his council.

On his left sat Mary, the Parish Clerk. Stephanie liked Mary, she was in her fifties, dark blonde hair with a natural curl. She sat behind her laptop efficiently, ready to take the minutes of the meeting. Mary was proficient at the job, she worked at the council offices, so she knew the legalities often better than Mr Grayling did, much to his annoyance it seemed.

Stephanie looked around the table... Mr and Mrs Cook ran the village shop. They'd been there for years, Stephanie remembered living in Hibaldton as a small child before her parents moved to Rigby. Her mum used to give her 50p to buy a bag of sweets and Mrs Cook was always so patient with her while she decided which sweets to choose.

Reverend Pierce was sitting next to them. He'd been a vicar at the church for a long time, and even though Stephanie didn't go to church often, she had been to a few sermons. Stephanie thought he was amusing. He often had a cheeky glint in his eye but now she noticed how old he was getting. He was becoming deaf and he looked like he was getting ready for a nap.

Next to the reverend sat Mrs Moore.

Stephanie was wishing she hadn't turned up as she never stopped moaning and it always ended up being about dog mess. She obviously wasn't an animal lover. She probably would make a good, wicked witch for a Wizard of Oz play, if the amateur dramatic group ever needed one.

Across the table from Stephanie, sat John Barry of Barry farm, then a couple of empty chairs…where was Sam Proctor? He only missed a meeting when he was harvesting his crops.

Just as Stephanie was wondering this, the door opened, and in he walked… or rather in walked his son, Mark Proctor!

Stephanie's stomach did a somersault as Mark strolled into the room and sat down opposite her. Everyone looked surprised to see him.

Mark was tall, with short, black hair. Stephanie noticed how his shoulders were broader than they used to be, and he obviously took care of himself. His face was just as handsome as she remembered.

Mark smiled easily at the Chairman and gave his father's apologies.

"You'll have to put up with me I'm afraid as my dad's not feeling too great tonight. In fact, you'll all be seeing more of me from now on as I'm taking more of an active role on the farm now."

This was aimed straight at John Barry who looked very uneasy and shifted in his seat. Stephanie looked on curiously, she didn't really have anything to do with the farms, but everyone knew that the two families didn't get on.

"Well send our best regards Mark, and welcome back to the village," Mr Grayling announced.

"Now first on the agenda is the disastrous plan for new housing in Hibaldton. I think we can all agree that something needs to be done to prevent so many people entering our small, sleepy village, and I have been making some noise at the council to investigate. So, fear not!"

His fist hit the air dramatically and set off a discussion amongst everyone. Rosie, Angela and Ben were sat on Stephanie's left. They ran the Village Voice, the village newsletter which came out every other month. Stephanie usually avoided them at that time as they always asked for help posting out the leaflets. Maybe Stephanie would try again to persuade them to just do a digital version, bring it into the 21st Century.

Angela spoke up, "I'm really worried about the open land behind my house. When we moved here, we came to live in a village, not a town. I don't want my lovely view to become a view of other people's gardens!"

"What about the field next to my road?" added Rosie, "There's a rumour of them squeezing 20 houses into there. Our village can't take all that extra traffic."

"Modern houses don't seem to have gardens anymore." Ben added.

"I don't believe you're thinking about everyone Rosie." Mr Cook raised his arm to get attention.

"Our shop has not been doing well since they built that supermarket. You know that we could do with the extra trade."

Mrs Cook nodded shyly, and everyone looked quite guilty as they all shopped at the supermarket now and then.

It was John Barry's turn to join in the debate.

"Lots of people have said to me that they want to have new housing in the village. There's lots of opportunities it could bring."

"Like what?" Angela and Rosie demanded.

"Well…the local shops, people would spend more money there. Not to mention the hairdressers and the school gets more money for every child they take on."

He turned his face towards Stephanie for

support.

"If there's room," Stephanie replied.

Reverend Pierce said, "It's also true that a lot of young people who grew up in the village are finding it hard to stay here. We do need some houses for first time buyers."

The debate raged on, and everyone started to discuss the topic amongst themselves until Mary put her hand up.

"May I suggest something Chairman?"

She was careful to not undermine Mr Grayling.

"How about if I write up the pros and cons mentioned tonight, and I could share the document for everyone to see ready for the next meeting. Also.."

"Yes, yes . Mary, make sure you write up these points mentioned. Why don't you put the pros in one column, and the cons in another so we can see them clearly? I would like you to email it to me first though."

Mr Grayling took control of the situation.

"Certainly," Mary agreed.

"I'm not sure it's necessary though. I can see that most people here agree that it would be against our interests for the village to grow any further. Our primary school is full, our surgery won't be able to cope, the roads are too narrow… we do not have the capacity. As your Chairman, it is my job to protect the village."

He seemed to grow in height that Stephanie thought he took his position seriously.

"Right- any other business?" Bryan enquired.

Reverend Pierce coughed, "As you all know, our church is still needing some repairs so does anyone have some ideas for raising money?"

"Wasn't the clock tower rebuilt last year?" Angela asked.

"Pardon?" The reverend lent forward cupping his hand round his ear.

"Last year!" Angela repeated a bit louder.

"Beer? Well… I suppose we could have a Beer Fest is that what it's called? That should raise some money," he chuckled.

There was that glint in his eye, Stephanie was sure he'd done that on purpose although he did have a hearing aid.

Mrs Moore turned to him, "Oh really? I, I hardly think that's an appropriate thing to do in a church do you Reverend? Perhaps tea and scones would be better."

Lisa leaned in and whispered, "Not if you're making them."

To which Stephanie had to stifle a giggle and ended up choking. She elbowed her friend in the ribs and then caught Mark looking at them.

Mark turned away and then added,

"Proctor Farms would be happy to make a donation Reverend if that helps. Though I think a Beer Fest would be a popular idea in the Summer. Maybe it could be held here Chairman?"

"Ooh yes," Ben was getting excited, he was always enthusiastic when it came to events. "We could have a marquee and a barbecue! There could be bunting all around, I can see it now. Shall we put that in the Village Voice?"

"All in favour for a Beer Fest to raise money for the church?"

Mr Grayling looked around the room at the raised hands.

"Yes ok, put that down Mary and add that a date is yet to be decided."

"Anything else?"

"Err, of course Barry Farm will match whatever Proctor's is giving."

"Oh thank you." Reverend Pierce smiled.

A shrill voice made Stephanie jump, "Well, …I would like to bring up the situation of dog mess on our footpaths."

"Mrs Moore strikes again," everyone thought.

"Furthermore, I am almost certain that someone is doing it right in front of my house every day!"

Lisa snorted at that comment but everyone else managed to control themselves.

"There are too many dogs in this village, if you ask me. I'm not being funny but, doggers should be held accountable!"

Stephanie and Lisa didn't dare look at each other, or that would have been it!

"Now, now, Mrs Moore, don't get yourself upset. We have signs around the village but what else can we do?" The reverend patted her arm.

"We could put another reminder in the Village Voice?" Rosie suggested, "and talking of the Village Voice…we do need some volunteers to hand out the leaflets."

"Why don't we just do an online version this time, try it out?" Stephanie suggested.

There were a few murmurs of agreement. Mrs Moore tutted, "Oh Stephanie but not everyone has a computer you know."

"We could have a few copies in the shop. What do you think Mrs Cook?"

Stephanie was pleased with her own idea, that would be another reason for people to go to the shop she thought.

Mr and Mrs Cook agreed, but Rosie, Angela and Ben thought that they should still post them.

The next hour was taken up with discussions

about the upcoming Beer Fest, money issues and the next month's bookings for the Village Hall. It was good that the hall seemed very popular.

It was difficult for Stephanie to stop herself from yawning until Mary brought up that she'd noticed an increase in the amount of traffic using the tracks down to the river. Mr Grayling said that it was just another reason why the village didn't need an increase in housing. "Too much traffic and people about. "

He promised he would look into it then he briskly adjourned the meeting until next time.

2
NOTHING'S A SECRET IN A SMALL VILLAGE

"Wow that got a bit heated." Lisa recalled as they sipped their drinks at The Old Mill pub.

They sat at a small table by the window, Stephanie sat with her back to the door.

"Mr Grayling seemed to be keen to finish. Do you think he couldn't wait to drink his pint?" Lisa wondered out loud.

She nodded over to him at the corner table. The pub was quiet, which was normal for a Wednesday night.

"Who's that man sitting with him?" Stephanie asked.

"I've never seen him before." Lisa peered over Stephanie's shoulder." They look like they're having an in-depth discussion though. Now they're looking at an iPad."

"Probably council business."

They couldn't see him clearly, he had his head down and was wearing a black wool hat and a black jumper, he didn't look a council type. Stephanie looked round, he was huge she noticed, with massive hands.

Stephanie was busy making up amusing reasons as to what Mr Grayling could be meeting him about. Maybe he was having an affair... or he could be meeting with his personal trainer. The guy looked like ex- SAS , maybe Mr Grayling had hired a secret agent. Stephanie looked at Lisa and saw her friend's eyes grow wide. She looked round thinking they were standing behind her, but instead it was Mark Proctor looking down at her with amusement dancing in his brown eyes.

"Gossiping about the neighbours, are we?" he laughed and he sat right down at their table.

Lisa nearly choked on her cider.

"So, what did you think about that meeting then?" he asked.

Mark sat back in his chair smiling, as if he'd never been away.

Lisa shrugged, "Just a typical Hibaldton council meeting. You should have been to the last one when Old Mrs Jackson was there. She got so animated that she fell off her chair and her false teeth flew out across the table."

"Mrs Jackson the organist? She's not still playing in the church is she, she must be getting on a bit!"

Lisa nodded," She must be a hundred and two and yes she still sings too. Poor Reverend Pierce. I've noticed that he turns his hearing aid off when the hymns start."

"Then forgets to turn it back on again, and shouts into the microphone," Stephanie added.

They all laughed, and Stephanie looked at Mark and wondered what he was doing back home.

"It was generous of you to offer a donation to the church." Stephanie smiled, "and to back up the Reverend's idea for a Beer Fest."

"Well, it sounds like a good plan, just what this village needs," Mark replied.

"I'm sure you must find it very boring here compared to busy London," Stephanie said.

Stephanie realised she'd given away the fact that she knew where he had been living and regretted it. She didn't want him to think she had been talking about him.

Lisa came to the rescue," Well you know, nothing is a secret in a small village."

"I'm surprised the village hasn't got anything more interesting to talk about, and it's not a secret anyway." Mark leant forward as he spoke.

"And since I've returned… I've realised that this place has recently got a lot more attractive."

Stephanie wasn't sure if that was aimed at her, but she could feel the heat rising in her face all the same.

"Err would anyone like a drink, my shout."

Stephanie stood up, far too quickly.

Lisa smiled and looked at her watch, "Oh, Martin will be wondering where I am, I should go."

"Oh just one more," Stephanie pleaded.

She didn't want to be left alone with Mark but on the other hand she didn't want to leave. The chemistry she had felt between them was surprisingly still there and she hadn't felt this way since Pete, her ex- boyfriend. Actually, she realised, she'd not felt this way even with Pete. Lisa agreed to one more cider and before Stephanie could say anything, Mark was steering her towards the bar.

Stephanie stood at the bar and could see the reflection of Mark next to her in the mirror. He was standing very close she thought. She could feel their shoulders touching and could smell his aftershave.

"What would you like, Steph?"

What would she like? She would like not to feel so nervous and for her legs to not be so wobbly. She frowned, trying to take control of her senses.

"A glass of white wine please…I'll be just a minute."

Stephanie left and headed for the bathroom. She just needed to have a moment to think, and check to see what she looked like in the mirror.

In the toilets she bumped into Mary, the clerk from the meeting.

"Oh hello Mary. Great idea by the way, you know to share the pros and cons," Stephanie gabbled, still feeling flustered from thinking about Mark.

"Thank you, Stephanie. Are you ok? You look flushed."

"Oh yeah, just concerned about the new houses, you know." Stephanie pulled herself together.

"Well, I didn't get a chance to say much at the meeting, but I wanted to say that I've been looking into the plots of land around the village that have planning requests. Would you be interested in what I find out? Did you know that there are eleven land plots requesting to be changed for housing development?"

"Wow, really? That's a lot."

"Hmm, you know the strangest thing is that some of the plots are owned by different people who don't even live in the village. Would you like me to let you know what I find out?"

"Er, yes please Mary. Thanks."

"You should come round for a cup of tea sometime. My house is easy to spot, it's on East Street, the cottage with the yellow door."

"Oh, I know which one you mean, the cottages look so lovely," Stephanie remarked.

"Yes, they have a lot of history you know. The cottage next door to mine used to be the local police station."

"Really? I would love to come and visit, thank you Mary."

"I'll speak to you later then. Good night," she called as she headed out through the bar.

Stephanie looked in the mirror and groaned. She tried to tame her auburn, shoulder length, thick hair and took a deep breath. Ok she felt much better after talking to Mary.

Back in the bar she saw Mark talking to someone, but when she arrived, he turned and handed her the drink. Stephanie took a sip and looked at Mark.

"So Steph, how are you these days? I hear you're teaching in the village."

"Now look who's listening to gossip." Stephanie teased. "Yes, I love it here actually. It's close to mum and dad in Rigby, and I have my own house."

"Where do you live?"

"On Field View, near the end, overlooking the fields."

Mark looked a bit surprised. "Oh, then that makes us practically neighbours."

"Well, your Proctor's farm is on the other side of the field. It is a big field," Stephanie pointed out.

They started walking back to the table.

"So, are your mum and dad ok? You mentioned they needed your help."

There was a pause, then Mark carefully replied," Dad is getting older and more stressed lately shall we say. I decided to come back and see to things and bring him into the 21st century."

"It must be stressful running a farm."

"Well, it would be less stressful if we didn't have such a difficult neighbour... John Barry is a piece of work."

They sat down with Lisa and Stephanie could tell that he didn't want to talk about it, so she changed the conversation.

"It seems like a long time since we saw each other."

Mark looked thoughtful,

"Too long," he admitted.

"I'm surprised you remember me," Stephanie said sipping her wine.

Mark drew his eyebrows together, "Of course I remember you. We went to the same primary school until you moved to Rigby, and then we went to the same secondary school."

"But you were a year above me, " Stephanie said.

What she didn't say was she was surprised he noticed her at all. Since she was about sixteen, and Mark was in sixth form, Stephanie had fancied him like mad. Lisa was the only person who she had confided this to.

"You were in the same year as my husband, Martin," Lisa said.

"Oh you and Martin got married, that's great." Mark smiled.

"Yeah, we've been married 9 years now." Lisa replied.

"Wow. I got on well with Martin, we should all get together sometime."

"That sounds great, doesn't it Steph?"

Lisa looked at Stephanie with a twinkle in her eye. Stephanie could feel Mark looking at her, she nodded and tried to stay cool.

"Hmm yeah," she smiled and gulped a drink of wine.

Stephanie wasn't sure whether Mark was

including her in this scenario, but he seemed happy about it.

After another hour went by Lisa looked at her watch. She had messaged Martin and he was picking her up outside the pub.

"Oh there's my ride," she said looking out the window.

Lisa stood up and said goodbye, giving Stephanie a hug.

Mark and Stephanie stayed for longer. The pub was almost empty by now, but they didn't seem to notice. They chatted about the past 8 years, mainly what Stephanie had been doing. She told him about her ex. Pete, and how they had grown apart. It was easy to talk to Mark and he genuinely seemed to be interested. The time flew by, and before they knew it, it was closing time.

"Oh my goodness, I didn't realise it was so late," Stephanie said as they were putting on their coats.

Mark chuckled, "How are you getting home?"

"I walked here."

"Come on then, I'll walk you home."

They finished their drinks and stepped out into the cold, night air. As they walked, Stephanie told Mark about the strange encounter with Mary.

"That does seem a high number to be turned into houses. Well, it's not on our land. I think I might ask about and see what I can find out."

"Mary said she was going to let me know. It sounds like she's doing a bit of detective work herself."

"Really?" Mark seemed surprised.

The journey home seemed over far too quickly, and before she knew it, they were standing outside her front door.

"It was nice seeing you again Mark. Thanks for seeing me home."

"It's my pleasure."

Mark took a step closer and pushed back a strand of hair from Stephanie's face. It sent a tingle through her body as she looked up at his face. For a moment they stood, and Stephanie could see the line of his jaw under the streetlamp. She could hear his breath catch as he looked deep in thought then he took a step back.

"I'll see you later… goodnight and sweet dreams."

Stephanie could see the amusement in his smile, but also something else in his voice.

"Good night, Mark."

Stephanie opened her front door and watched him turn and walk slowly away. She waited, and he turned to look once more, then she closed the door.

"Wow! Did that just happen?"

Stephanie leant against the door, her heart beating fast. As she got ready for bed, she remembered the times at secondary school, when she had passed him in the corridors she had always felt a flutter whenever he smiled at her. Stephanie and her friends would hang out at the park in Rigby at the weekend and Mark would sometimes show up.

There was also the school disco! Stephanie was in her first year at sixth form and Mark was in his final year. She had begun to see more of him then since she shared the same common room. Stephanie remembered a disco which had been held in the hall. She was sitting, talking to her friends, when Mark had walked towards her and she thought he was going to ask her to dance but then a girl had grabbed him and pulled him away. Stephanie sighed. She felt like a teenager all over again. Except she wasn't, she told herself.

Stephanie slowly walked upstairs. She'd had boyfriends, she'd been in a serious relationship that had lasted a year! It was over now. He had got a job in Wales and Stephanie didn't want to move that far away. Stephanie brushed her teeth as she thought about it. She hadn't really missed him when he moved away, so it had turned out for the best. She slid between the sheets and planned on having sweet dreams-about Mark.

3
WHEN IS THE RIGHT TIME TO INTRODUCE THE PARENTS?

The next morning, Stephanie was bleary eyed and couldn't concentrate. She ran around the house, gathering her things with a slice of toast in her mouth. She was just thinking of taking the car to work, when there was a knock at the door. Nobody usually knocked that early in the morning! For a moment her heart stopped at the possibility it could be Mark. Could it? She rushed to the door and opened it nervously.

"Hiya!" Lisa burst in excitedly. "I just couldn't wait to find out what happened last night. Did he walk you home? You look very tired! Did he come in?" Lisa gasped.

"No!" Stephanie cried indignantly. "But… there was something."

"Tell me everything. Don't leave anything out."

They both travelled to school talking about the night before. Lisa decided that Mark was interested in Stephanie. He had spent the whole evening with her after all.

At lunch time they ate their sandwiches in the classroom so they could continue the conversation.

"Stop plotting to get us together Lisa. I don't think he's interested in me."

"Well, he did say he was going to be around for a while….so you never know…" Lisa shrugged. "We need to find out more about him. Does he have a girlfriend? I don't think he's married; we would have heard about that. What did he tell you about himself?"

Stephanie thought about it and realised that he hadn't revealed much about himself.

"He didn't mention having a girlfriend," Stephanie said.

"Well then. He seemed keen for us to go out as a foursome."

"I don't know for sure if that's what he meant…but we did get on really well."

"I think you two have got the hots for each other. You can tell."

Stephanie stared at her friend and they both burst out laughing.

"Right, I need to stop thinking about him

now. Talk about something else."

Stephanie put her lunch box in her bag. She remembered her encounter with Mary in the pub and for the remainder of the break they discussed what that was all about. Eleven plots of land up for planning permission. Where would they be?

"We could do with a map of the village," Lisa said thoughtfully.

"Mary told me that she would let me know what she finds out. I wonder what she's looking for?" Stephanie wondered. "All the plots are owned by different people outside the village. I don't see what there is to find out. "

With that the bell rang in the playground. The afternoon was going to be netball, which Stephanie was glad about. It would do the children good to run around in the playground, and it would be good for Stephanie too. The weather was chilly, she noted, but the sun was out.

"Get changed into your PE kits and wear your jumpers!" she raised her voice to the children who were busy taking off their coats and grabbing their PE bags off the hooks.

By the time Stephanie had finished for the day, she was exhausted and longed for a nice hot bath.

#

The weekend soon arrived. Saturday was taken up with shopping for food, tidying the house and doing the washing. Stephanie was just folding some clothes on the dining table when her phone rang, it was her mum.

"I was just checking that you're still coming over for lunch on Sunday," her mum said.

" I come over every Sunday, I would have let you know if I wasn't," Stephanie replied rolling her eyes.

"Don't roll your eyes at me Stephanie, I'm just checking."

How did her mum know? It must be a talent you acquire when you become a mother, Stephanie thought to herself.

"Sorry mum, you know I appreciate you cooking for me on a Sunday."

"It's my pleasure. You're my baby and you work so hard, it's the least I can do."

"Thanks mum."

"The butcher had a lovely piece of beef that wasn't too expensive, and I'll make Yorkshire puddings as usual, it will be ready for 12 o'clock."

"I promise I won't be late. Bye mum."

"Bye," her mum said and then hung up.

She walked over to the patio doors, it was

starting to get dark, and she could see lights on in the farmhouse at the opposite end of the field.

"What are you doing right now?" Stephanie said out loud as she thought about Mark and his family. She wondered what the situation was with them and the Barry farm. Why was John Barry 'a piece of work'?

Stephanie decided to spend the evening watching a film, she chose an easy rom-com film and opened a bottle of red wine. The week had been quite eventful, she decided, and when the film ended, she went to bed.

#

The clock showed 9:00 in the morning when she opened her eyes. She sat up and decided that she felt like a jog before she went to her parents' house. She sprang out of bed, got into her leggings and sports bra, which was always a struggle, and chose her favourite top. It was pale blue and had writing across the front which read, "It's time to hit the gyn." She matched it with some pale blue socks and her trainers.

She started with a brisk walk while choosing her gym playlist on her phone. Buds in her ears she broke into a slow jog. Ok so she hadn't jogged for a while, it was more of a walk, jog, walk thing.

At the end of the road, she stopped. Which way should she go? She could either go up towards the village hall or turn right and run down the lane. Normally she would go down the lane, but that went past Proctor's Farm and now she felt awkward about going that way. If Mark saw her, he'd think she was stalking him. Oh, this was so annoying, so, she turned left and jogged up past the village shop. There was a sporty red car parked outside that she'd not seen before, so as she walked past, she glanced in the window to see who it belonged to. Mark was at the counter talking to Mr Cook. Luckily, he didn't look round, but Stephanie sprinted past just in case he saw her. Round the corner, she stopped and gasped for breath. Hands on knees she slowed down her breathing before continuing around behind the church and back home.

She slowed down to a walk to cool down, and as she was nearly home, she felt a car slow down behind her. Stephanie turned her head to look, and a low, red sports car pulled up beside her. The passenger window rolled down so Stephanie bent down to peer into the car. Mark's wide grin caused Stephanie's breathing to speed up again and her pulse rate rise.

"I thought that was you," he laughed, "I was coming to see you anyway."

"Oh yeah?" Stephanie put her hands on her hips and tried to slow her breathing.

"You never gave me your number," Mark explained.

Stephanie noticed that his eyes were taking in her close-fitting sportswear as she opened the car door and slipped into the seat beside him.

"Drive me home first before I collapse."

Mark laughed, "I take it you're not practising for a marathon."

"That would be a definite no."

Stephanie got out her phone from the pocket in her leggings, and Mark told her his number.

"So, what are you doing today?" he asked as he drove her home.

"It's Sunday. I usually go to my parent's house for roast dinner."

"They live in Rigby, don't they?" Mark asked.

"Yes," Stephanie replied cautiously.

"I remember your mum and my mum used to serve sandwiches at the village hall sometimes, at the cricket matches and fetes." Mark remembered.

"Oh yeah," Stephanie recalled, "I forgot that my mum knows your mum. I don't think they've been in touch for years though."

"You'll have to come over and see my parents, I bet mum would love to see you again," Mark said as he pulled up and parked.

Mark sat in the car, with his arm over the back of Stephanie's seat. Stephanie looked at him and longed to spend more time with him. Here he was talking about her seeing his parents, should she invite him? Stephanie thought about him meeting her mum, dad and grandma. She wasn't sure she was ready for him meeting them just yet.

"That would be nice, I'd love to see your mum again," Stephanie said.

"Well, I'll let you go to your parent's then," Mark said.

"Yes…"

Stephanie opened the car door and got out. Leaning in through the window she said, "When shall I see you again?"

"How about we go out for a meal next week? Do you like Indian?"

"Yep, I do," Stephanie nodded.

"I'll give you a ring."

"Ok, bye then," Stephanie smiled, "see you later."

Once inside, Stephanie ran upstairs and flopped back on her bed, her heart pounding. She listened to the sound of his car driving away and wished that she could have invited him inside. She had to get ready to go to her parent's anyway, her mum would kill her if she didn't turn up for lunch.

#

After a shower, she pulled on her jeans and a comfy jumper and got into her car. It was a white Fiesta that she had bought new about four years ago. Her dad had persuaded her to buy a brand-new car because he didn't want her to break down, but the monthly payments were making her regret the choice. Still, she loved it and enjoyed driving.

"I'm not having a daughter of mine breaking down in the middle of nowhere. It's all country lanes around here, you'll never get a signal," her dad had said.

Stephanie pulled up outside her parent's house and walked in.

A delicious smell of cooking rose to meet her as she walked into the kitchen. Her mum was busy finishing the gravy, the table was set and grandma was already sitting down looking at the clock. They looked up at Stephanie.

"Hello," they both called.

Grandma lifted her cheek for a kiss and Stephanie bent down. Grandma Bettie was small and thin, with short curly, light blue hair. She had it done at the hairdressers every Thursday. She was seventy-six, and she had always looked young for her age, but her skin was getting wrinkly Stephanie noticed.

She then went over to give her mum a hug. Barbara was fifty five with shoulder length curly auburn hair.

"Can I give you a hand?" she asked her mum.

"You could take these dishes to the table and call your dad."

Stephanie put the dark blue dishes on the table and went to find her dad, Malcolm. He was sat in the living room doing a crossword. His short, black head bent over; his thick eyebrows scrunched in concentration. He looked up from the paper and smiled at his daughter.

"Hello Munchkin," he smiled, "back to the mad house are we?"

"I can't keep away." Stephanie laughed. "Come on, dinner's ready. Grandma's already sat there with her knife and fork in her hand."

"Oh, that crazy mother of your mum's is going to be the death of me."

"Oh, stop moaning dad," Stephanie walked with him into the kitchen.

They all sat at the table and grandma lifted her plate.

"Come on Barbara, I'm starving. Can I have some beef and two Yorkshire puddings this time."

"Leave some for us," Malcolm tutted.

They all started eating when Stephanie's mum looked at Stephanie and asked, "So what's new?"

"Nothing," Stephanie replied.

"You look different," her mum noticed.

"No I don't," Stephanie started to feel self-conscious, "Why?"

"Barbara's right, have you got a new boyfriend?" Grandma Bettie joined in.

"What? How? Who told you that? No!" Stephanie gasped.

Stephanie's mum and grandma laughed as if they shared a secret.

"An old friend rang me up this morning, you know Beverley Proctor. She told me that her son Mark is back home."

Stephanie picked up a glass of water and had a drink. Wow, news certainly travels fast in between villages.

"Yes, he was at the Parish Council meeting on Wednesday. I didn't know you were still in touch with his mum."

"I haven't heard from her in ages. It was nice to hear from her again." Stephanie's mum said as she poured more gravy on her plate.

There was a pause while they all continued eating.

"So…did she say anything about me?" Stephanie asked trying not to sound too interested.

"She said that Mark seemed excited about seeing you again," Stephanie's mum grinned.

"Who's this Mark?" Stephanie's dad asked.

"Oh, we just met at the pub after the meeting, and we're going out for a meal next week," Stephanie told them.

"Is he good-looking?" Grandma Bettie asked.

Stephanie's dad rolled his eyes, "Trust you to ask that," he said.

"Well, our Stephanie deserves the best," Grandma Bettie insisted.

"Everyone has different tastes," Stephanie's mum said.

"I can see that," Grandma Bettie nodded towards Stephanie's dad who looked up from his plate.

"What's that supposed to mean?"

"Would you like your pudding in the front room love?" Stephanie's mum interrupted and gave her mum a sharp stare.

Sunday dinners were usually entertaining, Stephanie thought. Poor mum was usually the referee intervening between her dad and grandma before they jumped at each other's throats. Dad put up with her grandma because he knew she needed them, but he wasn't keen on her moving in when her husband died. Grandma Bettie didn't really want to leave her house either, but she was finding it difficult to manage on her own, so that's when Stephanie bought her grandma's house in Hibaldton and grandma moved in with Stephanie's parents. Grandma Bettie deliberately wound Malcolm up though, there were times when Stephanie was worried that her Grandma might end up living with her. Not that she didn't love her grandma, but she was a force of nature that she couldn't deal with 7 days a week.

It was 5 o'clock and it was starting to get dark. They had enjoyed a game of cards; grandma had won for the forth time and Stephanie's dad was grumbling that he was sure she was cheating.

"Lucky at cards, unlucky in love," Grandma Bettie sighed.

She sat back and crossed her arms with a sly grin on her face. Stephanie stood up before her dad could say any more.

"I'll help you tidy the kitchen mum."

"Oh, it's already taken care of love. You get

on home, I don't want you driving home in the dark."

Stephanie kissed everyone goodbye and gave her mum an extra hug as she was handed the leftovers in a casserole dish.

"Thanks mum," Stephanie called as she got into her car and drove home.

#

Monday went by in the usual busy way, and it was home time before there was any chance of thinking about Mark again. Stephanie was sat at her desk when she heard her phone ping. She reached into her bag to look and saw a message had popped up.

"Hi."

Stephanie didn't recognise the number… could it be from Mark?

She typed back, "Hi."

She waited. She probably should have asked who it was.

"Shall we go for that meal? How about Wednesday?"

Stephanie's pulse rate was racing, she looked up as Lisa entered the classroom. Lisa walked over and tried to look at the message, but Stephanie picked up her phone.

"Message from Mark?" Lisa enquired casually.

"He's asking me to go out for a meal on Wednesday," Stephanie tried to sound calm.

"You are going, aren't you?" Lisa urged.

Stephanie started to type into the phone, reading it out loud so her friend could hear.

"OK that would be nice…"

"You can't put that!" Lisa grabbed the phone and started to type.

Stephanie was appalled and tried to grab the phone back, but Lisa was too quick. She pressed send and gave it back with a smile on her face.

"What did you put?" Stephanie demanded, her face pale.

She looked at the message which read, "I can't wait to see you again. Pick me up at 7."

"Lisa!" Stephanie shouted, "What's he going to think?"

"He'll be happy you're looking forward to it. Don't you think you two have played enough games? You're adults now Steph."

They both looked at the phone to see what Mark would reply.

"Great! I'm really looking forward to it."

Stephanie held her breath as she read the message. She stared at it wondering if he meant it. Then dots appeared as he continued to type…

Stephanie and Lisa waited but they

disappeared.

"Send a love heart." Lisa suggested.

"Don't be silly, I don't want to scare him off." Stephanie switched the phone off and continued to mark her books.

"Well, I'm off then," Lisa said and walked over to the stock cupboard to get her coat. "Don't be scared to show him how you feel Steph, I think he really likes you."

Stephanie watched Lisa go and she looked out of the window. She could see the empty playground and the village beyond. She got her phone out once more and saved his number into her contacts. He hadn't sent anything else. She thought about what Lisa had said about not being scared to show him how she felt. Stephanie was usually more confident than she used to be as a teenager. He probably wasn't going to stay around for much longer anyway, she should just enjoy the company of an old friend and just see where it goes. The trouble was that when she was near him, her brain turned to mush and her body tingled. She breathed deeply at the thought of it and told herself to get a grip on her feelings. Wednesday was two days away for goodness sake.

4
THE FIRST DATE

Wow Wednesday came fast. How did that happen? Stephanie emptied her wardrobe and stood glaring at the heap of clothes on her bed. In the end she decided on jeans and a flowery top that did show a bit of cleavage. She chose a necklace with a heart pendant and hoop earrings. She just had time to hang her clothes up again when there was a knock on the door. She hadn't heard a car pull up.

She took a deep breath and gingerly walked downstairs.

She opened the front door and was surprised to see Grandma Bettie waving goodbye to a car.

"Grandma? What are you doing here?"

"Oh goodness, what a day I've had. I need to sit down dear."

Stephanie stood aside to let her in the house and watched her grandma sit down on the settee.

"I was hoping you would have made something to eat, I can't smell anything." Grandma Bettie said looking up at Stephanie. "You look nice dear, are you going out?"

Stephanie sighed and replied that she was expecting a friend to take her out for a meal.

"Ooooh is it that nice young man, what's his name?"

"Mark. Yes it is actually."

Stephanie was beginning to panic, she hadn't been expecting Mark to be introduced to her grandma just yet. She looked at her watch, it was 6:30 there probably was time to take her grandma back home, or she could text Mark and tell him she would meet him there. Yes, that was a good idea. Stephanie reached for her phone that was on the table and began to type..

"Sorry, change of plan. Can I meet you in Rigby? Taking my grandma home."

Stephanie grabbed her handbag and started to pull her grandma up from the settee.

"Come on grandma, I'm taking you home."

"But I've just got here," she replied obstinately.

"Why are you here? Is everything ok?"

Stephanie began to get worried, her grandma didn't usually just turn up like this.

"Yes, I'm fine. I've just been on a date with Fred. He lives near the fish and chip shop and instead of him driving me home, I said he could drop me off here. He still has his driving licence, but between you and me, he's as blind as a bat."

"What? Should he be driving then? Never mind, come on grandma, I need to take you home because I'm going on a date." Stephanie was starting to think that the date had already got off to a bad start and maybe she should just call it off.

Grandma Bettie sprang to her feet suddenly and started off out the door.

"Come on then, why didn't you say so? I can give you some pointers on the way…"

Stephanie rolled her eyes and they got into her car.

Back at her parents' house, Stephanie walked into the kitchen to see them eating at the table.

"Stephanie, what a nice surprise," her mum cried when she saw them walk in. "Would you like something to eat?"

Grandma Bettie almost pushed Stephanie out of the way.

"Yes, I'm starving. That old goat took me out for lunch, but we only had sandwiches at the Memorial Club. I think I need to find someone a bit more sophisticated like Stephanie has now."

"What does she mean?" Stephanie's dad wanted to know.

"Oh, she must mean Mark, he is a nice young man. Is he your boyfriend now?" Barbara asked.

Stephanie stood there, not knowing what to say when there was a

knock at the door. Everyone froze.

"Who could that be?" Barbara asked surprised.

"Are you giving me that Yorkshire pudding or not?" Grandma cared more about food than who was at the door.

"I'll go," Stephanie volunteered.

She opened the door, and to her surprise there stood Mark smiling.

"Hello."

"What are you doing here?" Stephanie asked.

"Well…you said to meet you in Rigby…"

Mark started to look less confident. He put his hand through his hair and continued, "and as I hadn't told you where we were going, I thought I'd try here."

Before Stephanie could answer, she felt her mum behind her.

"Oh come on in, Bev Proctor's boy isn't it?"

"Yes Mrs Rhodes, Mark. How are you?"

"Oh we're fine. We're just having dinner if you'd like to join us."

"Oh but we're going out…" Stephanie mumbled, trying to stop her mum.

"That's very kind of you, if you're sure," Mark grinned shyly.

They walked into the kitchen and another plate was brought out for Mark.

"Oh it's no trouble at all, isn't that right Malcolm?"

Stephanie's dad eyed Mark suspiciously, "So I take it you're a friend of Steph's are you?"

"Yes, we've known each other for years and just recently met again." Mark reached over to shake his hand. "I'm Mark Proctor sir, Sam and Bev Proctor's son," he explained.

Stephanie's mum gave him a plate full of food.

"I was so pleased when your mum rang me, it's been a long time since we've seen each other. Now when did we used to help at those cricket matches? Malcolm you'll know."

Stephanie's dad was busy eating and not paying any attention.

"This looks delicious, thank you." Mark said.

Stephanie sat there, it felt like a dream. Usually, she dreamed about teaching a class where she had no control whatsoever…this was something similar.

"Well call me Barbara and this is Malcolm

and Stephanie's grandma Bettie."

Grandma Bettie and Malcolm looked like they were having a fight over the last Yorkshire pudding.

"But didn't you book a table?" Stephanie asked Mark.

"Well, I didn't think I'd need to as it's not busy so it's ok, we can eat here."

"Of course you can eat here. It's roast chicken tonight and I always make too much, don't I Malcolm?"

"You need to, the amount Bettie eats."

"There's nothing wrong with having a good appetite," Grandma Bettie explained waving her fork in the air.

"Some of us can eat and not put on weight…" she pointed her fork towards Malcolm's stomach, "and some of us need to exercise."

Mark spoke before Stephanie's dad had time to react, "I should take up running again. I never seemed to have the time in London, I could go running with you Steph."

Stephanie nearly choked on her food, and the rest of the family looked surprised.

"Stephanie gets out of breath going up the stairs," her dad laughed.

"I exercise sometimes," Stephanie defended

herself.

"I didn't know you were that fit Steph," Barbara said proudly.

"About time," Malcolm said waving his potato on the end of his fork.

Mark laughed and Stephanie glared at him.

"Well, he's very good-looking Stephanie," Grandma piped up, "I wish I had a boyfriend like that."

"Huh, that would be a sight to see," Malcolm mumbled under his breath.

Stephanie wished the ground would swallow her up! She looked at Mark and mouthed, "Sorry."

Mark smiled and tucked into his dinner. Stephanie tried to eat, but her stomach was in knots. Here was Mark Proctor, sitting next to her, eating dinner with her parents. She sneakily looked up at him, and he seemed to be enjoying himself.

"So young man, do you work with your dad then?" Malcolm asked.

He might as well have asked if he could support his daughter. Stephanie squirmed in her seat.

"I am, at the moment, but I do have a job in London. I'm a financial consultant for a firm, and I'm working from home, here, for now."

"I expect your girlfriend is missing you then," Barbara said.

Stephanie groaned and put her hand up to her face. Grandma looked like she was enjoying this. "This is better than Coronation Street this is," she said with her mouth full. Grandma Bettie always spoke her mind and had no filter whatsoever.

"I don't have a girlfriend at the moment," Mark replied looking at Stephanie and then back to Barbara. "Not yet anyway…May I have some more mashed potatoes?"

Barbara gushed, "Oh please do!" and passed him the bowl.

"So do you guys have any more questions to grill him with?" Stephanie asked. She was so embarrassed, but at least she had found out more about him without having to ask him herself.

"I expect your parents are glad to have you back at home again," Barbara continued.

"I don't live with my parents."

Stephanie looked at him, surprised. She had presumed he was living on Proctor's farm.

Mark turned to Stephanie. "Do you know the house at the end of the lane past my dad's farm? It was built about two years ago - at the end of the airfield?"

Stephanie nodded. She had noticed it being built when she went for walks and wished that she lived there. It was a big house with plenty of land around it, she could see it from her house. "Is that your house?"

"Yes, I decided to build it as an investment. I'd thought about renting it out, but now I'm glad I didn't. It has some furniture but it's not quite a home yet. You should come visit."

"Er yeah that would be nice."

Stephanie's dad stood up and muttered something about finishing his crossword and left the kitchen. Stephanie's mum made an excuse about leaving and told them not to clear up, she'd do it later. Grandma sat there staring at Mark.

"So, how are you, Bettie?" Mark asked her. That was the worst thing he could have asked Stephanie shook her head.

"Oh… I'm not very well. I know I don't look it, but I'm over seventy you know. It's my bowels, I can't keep off the toilet in the morning…"

Stephanie stood up and grabbed Mark's arm.

"I'm sure Mark doesn't want to hear about that grandma! Anyway, err, shall we go for a walk?"

Stephanie was determined to rescue the

evening. As first dates go- this was probably the worst one Mark had ever been on.

"I'm really sorry," she whispered. "She speaks her mind."

"It's ok," Mark laughed, "I like your family."

"Then you must be crazy too."

She lifted her coat off the peg and Mark helped her into it.

"Shall we walk along the river?" He asked as he reached for his jacket.

Stephanie agreed and felt relieved as they walked into the night air.

They slowly walked along the street.

"How did you know where my parents live?" Stephanie suddenly realised.

"We're right next to our old secondary school. Over there, the bus to Hibaldton used to stop, and I would sit at the front on the top deck. I often used to see you going home."

"I didn't know that," Stephanie said quietly.

"There's a lot you don't know about me," Mark replied.

They stopped and he bent down to kiss her on the lips. Just a soft, gentle kiss that felt warm and tingly. Then he slowly stood up, looking deep into her eyes and then took her hand on his and continued to walk on.

They walked in silence for a while, Stephanie

was feeling a bit shaken and didn't trust that she could speak. She could feel that Mark was also acting strangely. She looked up at him and he pulled her closer, wrapping his arm around her.

"I'm sorry our first date didn't turn out quite like you probably expected." Stephanie eventually said.

Mark looked at her and smiled, "It's true, it's not what I planned, but it's just as it should have been. I mean, being with you is like coming home."

He stopped walking to face Stephanie. They had reached the river, and the moonlight's reflection danced on the water's surface. He looked worried, as if he had offended her, and suddenly he looked nervous.

"What I mean is…God I'm usually much more in control than this…you have always had this effect on me."

He smiled and gently stroked back a strand of hair away from her eyes again which sent a tingle down Stephanie's spine.

"I…I didn't know," Stephanie began.

Mark pulled her closer and this time his kiss lasted longer. When their lips parted, they were both breathing heavily and Stephanie could see their breath against the cold air. She studied his lips, his straight nose, his dark eyes, she wanted to be able to remember every feature.

They wandered along the river and filled each other in on news of old friends and family. Mark's cousin was getting married in a year, his best friend from school, Stan, was going to be a dad and how much Mark had missed while he was away. Stephanie had spent four years training to be a teacher in Lincoln, she had succeeded in getting a teaching job in Hibaldton and in the recent five years she had bought her grandma's house. She revealed a little about her previous boyfriend and how he had moved to Wales. Stephanie realised that she didn't miss him and she was relieved that their relationship hadn't grown into anything more serious.

They turned around and started to walk back. Stephanie asked him about his life in London. Mark described his flat, it was above a row of shops, and it had a car park in the basement. He hardly drove it though as he used the underground to get everywhere he needed.

"Do you miss London?"

There was a pause before he answered.

"Yes and no. It all gets a bit much after a while, it's good to get away from it all."

"Are you under a lot of pressure at work?" Stephanie asked, interested to know more about him.

"It can be. I work for a company that advise businesses how to invest their money, so it's not the kind of job you can make mistakes in. I work with a good group though. We support each other and go out a lot to take our mind of things when things get rough, you know."

"Where do go out?"

"Do you know London?" he asked.

"Not really. I went with my mum and dad when I was a teenager to see the sights: Buckingham Palace, Tower of London, Leicester Square."

"I don't suppose they took you to Soho then," Mark laughed.

Stephanie chuckled, "No, not the kind of place to take a fifteen-year-old girl, at night anyway."

"You'd be surprised, anyway, we usually go to bars there and nightclubs. You'll have to come down with me and I'll show you around. There's a great Indian restaurant that is amazing. The local Indian community go there so you can tell its authentic food. Do you like Indian food?"

"Oh, I love Indian food, as long as it's not too spicy."

"I was going to take you for an Indian tonight actually, in Rigby."

"Sorry, we'll have to go another time then,"

Stephanie apologised.

"That's okay, I've enjoyed meeting your family properly, although I wasn't expecting it so soon," Mark laughed.

Stephanie and Mark wandered slowly along the main road until they came to her parents' house.

"We're here, I'd ask you in but…" Stephanie paused, hoping he'd take the hint.

"That's fine, I'll leave you to have some family time."

"See you soon then," Stephanie said awkwardly and started to walk up the drive.

"Wait," called Mark, "How about I show you around my parents' farm?"

"When?"

"Tomorrow?" Mark grinned, "Is it too soon?"

Stephanie flushed despite the cold air.

"No, tomorrow's fine. I can walk up after school."

"Great, see you there. Bye Steph."

"Bye."

Her mum and Grandma came rushing into the hallway eager to know what that was all about. Stephanie shrugged and told them that he'd only just returned, and she didn't really know what was happening either.

"I hope he doesn't break your heart!" Barbara warned.

"Great, thanks mum!"

"You just have a good time my girl! You're too young to be getting serious with boys. Play the field, keep them guessing. That's what I did before I met grandad."

Stephanie could hear her dad muttering again in the next room.

"Well thanks for a lovely meal again mum, but I should go now because I've got planning to do."

"You work so hard."

"It's ok mum. I just have to plan the week's maths lessons; it won't take long."

She hugged her mum and grandma.

"Bye dad!" Stephanie called through the wall and left to drive home.

5
THE PROCTOR'S FARM

On Thursday, Stephanie couldn't wait to talk to Lisa about the previous night.

The day was so busy that they didn't get to talk about it until home time.

Lisa groaned when she heard about Grandma Bettie arriving on her doorstep, and she gasped when Stephanie had texted Mark to meet her in Rigby. It took the whole day to recount all the details.

"When are you seeing him again?" Lisa asked.

"Today, he's going to show me round the farm."

Stephanie looked at the clock on the wall- 3:30, she started to pack away her laptop.

"I don't think my heart can take much more of this," Lisa continued, "just hurry up and sleep with him and get all that sexual tension out of the way."

Stephanie laughed, "Sexual tension is fun."

"Who are we talking about?" Tracy, the teacher next door, asked.

"How long were you standing there?" Stephanie asked nervously.

"long enough to know there's sexual tension and I wish I was having some." she laughed.

Tracy was a good laugh and entertained everyone in the staffroom with stories about her online dating experiences.

"We were just saying the same," Stephanie mumbled.

She grabbed her things and said she had to dash and gave a warning look to Lisa not to say anything. She didn't want her dating Mark to be the latest gossip around the village, not that it could be avoided she supposed.

#

Stephanie dropped her things round her house and then continued to walk down the lane. It was a single track road with houses on one side and fields on the other. The fields actually belonged to John Barry and Stephanie curiously looked over towards his farmhouse as she wandered past. She couldn't see anyone home. The houses on the right eventually gave way to fields . As the track came to an end, Stephanie turned right towards Proctor's Farm. A trickling stream flowed past and Stephanie unbuttoned her jacket to enjoy the Spring air around her. Buds were beginning to show on the branches and the noise of birds filled the air as they busily found nesting material. Stephanie looked across the fields towards her house, she could just make out the tree at the end of her garden. It was funny seeing it from the other side of the field, it looked so far away.

She turned into the farm's drive and nervously stopped. She didn't know whether to go to the door or walk down the side. Stephanie was just wondering what to do when the front door opened to reveal Bev, Marks's mum.

"Stephanie, hello dear. Come on in, they're in the office at the back."

Stephanie smiled and walked down the hall into a large kitchen. The house was surprisingly modern on the inside, with wooden floors and large glass windows which perfectly framed a lush garden lawn surrounded by trees and bushes.

"Wow you have an amazing garden Mrs Proctor." Stephanie said.

"Call me Bev and thank you. You should see it in the summer when the azaleas bloom. Would you like a cup of tea?"

"Oh yes thank you."

Stephanie stood leaning on the large, marble kitchen island. She looked around and admired the cream kitchen cupboards and the large American style fridge. Bev explained that Mark was in the office out in the garden with his dad and she would show Stephanie when her drink was ready. Next, she went on to talk about her memories of Stephanie, when she was little, playing at the village hall and how much she had grown up. Stephanie remembered playing with her friends while the cricket match was on. Mostly she remembered the tasty sandwiches and home-made cakes.

They walked outside with their cups of tea, down a path that led round the corner to a stone building.

Mark looked up as Stephanie walked in and his face it up.

"Just in time to rescue me," he beamed.

"Ah well, we've finished any way. Hi there trouble, it's good to see you again Stephanie." Mark's dad had a smile a lot like his son.

"Hello, I see you've been busy." Stephanie looked around.

There was a large desk, which nearly filled the room, and the desk was piled high with paper work and two computer monitors. In the corner stood filing cabinets and there were bookshelves full of folders and box files.

"Oh I hate paper work and computers even more. Thank goodness Mark's here to sort things out." Sam scratched his head and rubbed his chin.

"Come on, I'll show you round the place." Mark reached out for Stephanie's hand and guided her back outside.

They walked through the garden towards some trees, where a path led to a fishing lake. Stephanie had often walked to the lake but on the other side. A couple of swans glided over in hope of food.

"This is Bert and Gloria," Mark pointed out.

"Bert and Gloria?" Stephanie asked.

"I named them after my aunt and uncle," Mark shrugged and smiled.

"It suits them," Stephanie said and watched them swim off together.

"Who lives in the caravan?"

A large static caravan stood next to the lake, it looked like it had been there for years.

"Dave- my dad's farm manager. He's lived there for a few years now since he split up with his wife. It's handy that he lives there I suppose. He helps to look after the farm and keeps a check on people when they fish here."

Mark led Stephanie past the lake to farmland beyond.

"So, our land runs all the way down to the River Ancholme," Mark explained.

They walked along a dirt track and stopped at a huge barn. The barn was open and inside was a store of hay bales. In the distance Stephanie could see a tractor slowly moving up and down the field.

"That's Dave finishing spraying."

"What are you planting behind my house?" Stephanie asked.

"Wheat this year." Mark replied.

"Oh good, my favourite," Stephanie smiled as she told Mark how she loved to look out at the wheat in the summer.

Mark watched her with an amused look and walked closer to her so that she leaned with her back against a hay bale.

"Wheat's my favourite too, especially playing in the hay."

He picked a piece of hay and tickled Stephanie's neck gently with it.

She defensively put her hands up to his chest. He was wearing a denim jacket which was open, her hands lay on his white t-shirt and she could feel his warmth inviting her in. His eyes, which had been twinkling with humour, now grew dark with desire as he looked down into hers. His hand traced the line from her face, down her neck, brushed her breast to her waist. Stephanie groaned as he moved towards her, and her body melted into his. Her mouth reached up to find his and this time his kiss was hungry, hungry for more. She could feel him pressing against her, his hands reached behind her back, pulling at her blouse to feel the soft, hot bare flesh. Stephanie's skin had goosebumps as her passion rose, for a moment they completely forgot where they were.

A bark from behind Mark brought them back to reality and a black and white furry face pushed its way between them. They parted laughing and Mark reluctantly stepped back to reveal a gorgeous border collie, wagging his tail in excitement at a new visitor.

"Great timing Wendy." Mark knelt to stop her from jumping up. "Wendy this is Steph, Steph- this is my parent's dog Wendy."

"Aww she's so cute." Stephanie knelt down too, and Wendy lay on her back to have her tummy rubbed."

"Oh no, now she's here, she'll get all your attention."

Mark pretended to look disappointed, and Stephanie laughed. She tucked her blouse back into her trousers in time to hear his mum call them for tea. In a single bound, Wendy was up and urging them to go back to the house.

"I guess we'll have to continue where we left off another time."

Mark took Stephanie's hand and they walked back with Wendy running eagerly around them. Just before they went inside, Mark pulled a piece of hay from Stephanie's hair and winked. Stephanie tried to act normal when she sat down at the dinner table, but she was acutely aware how flushed she must have looked. Mr and Mrs Proctor must have noticed but they just smiled and started to dish out the food.

The evening was spent relaxed and happy. Stephanie told them how she had moved to Lincoln and now was living in her grandma's old house. Mark's mum and dad told Stephanie how their son had done so well at university. He had come up to help organise his dad and bring him into the 21st century.

"Did you see all the paperwork in the office?" Mark asked. "It's about time dad moved to a computer system."

Stephanie nodded and sympathised with Sam.

"My dad retired from mending boilers just as they were getting more complicated, he found it difficult to cope with the changes in technology." Stephanie explained.

"Trouble is Sam will never retire," Bev said patting her husband's leg, "you're too stubborn aren't you dear."

"Well, you don't need to dad, you can just take it a bit easier now I'm here," Mark said.

"How long will you be here for?"

Stephanie had asked the question before she had time to stop herself. But it was a good question that she had been dying to ask him.

"I don't know."

Mark looked a bit guilty and avoided her gaze. What did he mean by that?

Sam continued, "Our business partner, John Barry is just as technically ignorant as me, so it could take a while."

At the mention of John Barry's name, Mark's face looked more serious.

"If I have anything to do with it, he won't be your partner for much longer."

"Well…we'll have to wait and see." Bev laughed nervously, sensing the growing tension. "Now, who would like some rhubarb crumble?"

#

By time Stephanie got home, she had more time to ponder the situation. Well, at least he didn't lie and say he was staying for ever when he wasn't sure. At least she knew that her first instincts were sound. Once he had helped his dad out, he probably would be going back to London, his work and life was there after all. Stephanie tried to not feel hurt about it. If this thing between them grew into something more serious then would he ask her to move to London with him? Would she want to? It was a long time before Stephanie got to sleep that night.

6
A SHOCKING DISCOVERY

A week had gone by. It was Sunday and the half term holiday. Stephanie had just arrived home from dinner at her parent's house. She popped the box of leftovers in the fridge and pushed off her shoes. In the evenings, Mark and Stephanie had been regularly texting each other. It was just short conversations throughout the week as they were both so busy. Mark had gone away on a business trip. It was so frustrating not to be able to see him properly. He said that he was looking forward to taking her out where they could have a proper conversation. At times, Stephanie wished she had the guts to tell him what she wanted to do with him. It would involve getting naked and lots of hot sex! Oh how she wished he would come over. She was thinking of asking him when the phone rang.

Stephanie almost jumped out of her skin! She

looked around for her phone and found it on the breakfast bar.

She put it to her ear.

"Hello Stephanie, it's Mary."

"Oh -hello, how are you?" Stephanie breathed.

"I hope I'm not disturbing you on a Sunday."

Stephanie looked at the time, it was 6 o'clock.

"No not at all, I've just got back from my parents' house. Are you ok?"

"Yes I'm fine thank you, I've been very busy. The meeting at the Parish Council has been playing on my mind."

"Yes, the village is changing so fast. Everywhere you look there's new houses being built." Stephanie agreed.

"I know, and I hate to see so many people getting upset abut it. As I work for the council, I decided to look at the future requests for planning permission and to see who we will be up against."

"That's a good idea, are there many plans in the pipeline? I can't imagine where there's room for any more houses, and surely the farmland can't be built on can it?"

Mary laughed, "You'll be surprised. It's taken a while because I didn't want to be noticed, but I've managed to discover a common person involved."

Mary paused, as if building up the suspense.

"Well? Who is it?" Stephanie asked intrigued.

"John Barry," Mary replied. "He did well to hide his name but when I looked into the history of the landowners, I discovered that they were aliases of John. It seems he has been purchasing land over several years."

"Wow. That's a shock. What are you going to do?"

"I spoke to Bryan Grayling. Being the chairman of the parish, I thought he'd want to know."

"And what did he say?" Stephanie asked.

"He sounded shocked and said he would deal with it."

"What does that mean?"

"I don't know. He was very interested in everything I'd found out. I don't know what he can do though. I'm going to go for a walk down to the river. I'll be in touch."

"Ok then. Bye Mary, have a nice walk," Stephanie hung up.

"Wow, she's like Miss Marple," Stephanie giggled.

After sitting down with a glass of wine, Stephanie started thinking that Mark should know about John Barry- after all they were partners. She knew John Barry owned land down the lane, but she wasn't sure how far it went. There were a few farms in the area between Hibaldton and Rigby.

Plus, Stephanie was frustrated with Mark for not ringing her. What had he been doing all week? He had been very vague about it. One minute, he's acting all sexy, kissing her and flirting with her, and the next he's being mysterious and distant.

"Grr! Men!" Stephanie got up to refill her glass. She paced up and down, in and out of the living room.

"Right. I'm going to ring him. I'll ask him when he's coming home, and to come over when he gets here." She decided. She looked at her watch, it was nearly 7 o'clock. She emptied the glass and with trembling hands, she picked up the phone.

She waited while it rang.

"Hi," Mark answered.

He sounded happy.

"Hello." She tried to speak as casually as she could.

"I've been wanting to speak to you. I miss you." Mark replied.

His voice sounded soft and so sexy.

"I miss you too," Stephanie admitted.

"Oh yeah?"

"I have so many things I want to say… about us… but also about John Barry that I think you should know."

"Barry? What has he done now?" Mark sounded tense.

Stephanie regretted mentioning John Barry. She didn't need an excuse to ring him, why did she have to spoil the mood?

She continued, "I had Mary on the phone earlier and she told me it's John Barry that is buying up land in Hibaldton."

There was a pause and Mark's voice sounded tired.

"It honestly doesn't surprise me. It partly why I've been away. I'm negotiating a contract for our farm. It's a big contract Steph."

He sounded excited. "If I pull it off, it means we can be independent of him."

"That's great news! I know you'll succeed. Why do you dislike him so much?"

"Oh it's a long story. Our two families were close years ago and decided to join our farms in business. But then things started to go down hill and my dad and John fell out."

"That's a shame. "

"Yeah. It turned out John was spending money without consulting dad and selling parts of his land off without telling him. Anyway, I'm tired of talking business. What are you doing now?"

"I'm just downstairs with a glass of wine and missing you." Stephanie's voice almost became a whisper.

Silence…Stephanie could hear his breathing and wished she could see him. She could suggest a video call but she was feeling so nervous and emotional. She didn't want to do this over the phone.

"I wish I hadn't had to go away, but I should be able to come home by Friday. We haven't had time to really get to know each other, have we?"

"I know. I…to be honest I've had a bit too much wine…" Stephanie giggled and put her hand to her head. She'd been standing and suddenly needed to sit down. "I really want you to come home now."

"Oh god Steph! If this wasn't so important, I'd be there tonight. Believe me, I'm finding it hard not to race over but I've got a 9 o'clock meeting in the morning… You have no idea what an effect you have been having on me since we met. I can't stop thinking of you."

At those words, Stephanie wished she could jump into his arms.

"Are you going out tonight?" Stephanie asked.

"No, I'm sitting at my desk preparing my speech. I'm looking at my dad's records, crop yields and stuff. I've still got lots to do."

"I'll leave you to it then," Stephanie replied. "Good luck."

"Thanks, I'll need it. Goodnight Steph."

Stephanie hung up the phone and flung herself back on the settee. It was a good thing she'd finished her wine or it would have splashed all over.

"Oh my god! What are you doing to me?" She shouted. She stretched out against the cushions. Her body felt so hot and shivery, her head was spinning. She longed for Mark to be there, pressing his body against hers. Her body ached for his touch.

#

Stephanie spent the next couple of days being as busy as she could. Wednesday morning Stephanie was woken up in the early hours by a mysterious text message from Mary. Rolling over in bed, Stephanie reached out for the phone.

"I have something urgent to show you. When can you meet me?"

Stephanie sat up puzzled. She texted back, "Whenever you want."

She watched the dots as Mary typed.

"8 o'clock, outside the Village Hall, this morning."

Stephanie looked at the time. It was 5 am. What an Earth did Mary have to show her that was so urgent?

#

Stephanie walked up to the Village Hall. It was a sunny morning, but the breeze was icy. She walked briskly, turning right opposite the church, past the empty plot of land with the weeping willow tree. She paused at the corner to lean on the wall and say hello to two brown and white horses that were nibbling on the tufts of grass through the gate.

She crossed the road that led to Rigby and decided to walk across the playing field. She glanced over at Mr Grayling's house and noticed the fountain wasn't on. There was some building work going on though in the side garden. She tried to work out what it was, it looked like a stone summer house.

When she arrived at the car park, she looked for Mary. No sign of anyone. Stephanie walked over to the road and looked up and down. She was just in time to see the back of Mark's red sport's car turn rapidly at the junction and disappear into the village. What was he doing back? He said he was returning on Friday.

Stephanie returned to the car park and over to the door. That was when she noticed it was slightly open. Maybe Mary went inside.

Stephanie carefully opened the door and looked inside. It was very quiet and looked empty. She stepped into the entrance area and could see the door to the meeting room was open. Maybe Mary meant to meet in there. Stephanie walked to the room and looked inside. She peered around at the wall with the village plan, when something on the floor caught her eye. Something was wrong. Stephanie slowly walked forward. A dark coat was lying on the floor behind the chairs, a dark coat with … a pair of legs! Stephanie rushed over and knelt down next to Mary's body. Her face was slack, her eyes staring ahead, her mouth slightly open. Blood covered the side of her head and was wet on her face.

"M..Mary?" whispered Stephanie. Her hands trembled as she felt for a pulse on the side of her neck. She couldn't feel anything, but she felt warm.

"Oh no! Mary! Help! Someone help!"

Stephanie screamed. She jumped up and ran out of the room, into the car park. Wide eyed and panicking she ran straight into the caretaker, Frank.

"Oh thank God! It's Mary. She's...I think she's dead. Her body... in the meeting room."

"Come inside with me and ring the ambulance!" he insisted.

Stephanie answered all the questions on the phone while Frank did CPR. Nevertheless, Mary lay limp, an empty shell. Stephanie began to wonder how it had happened. It looked like Mary had hit her head but what on? There was blood on the right side of her head, and on the floor next to the table leg. There was also blood on the table leg... and on the corner of the table. Did she fall back and hit her head? What made her fall? Did she trip over something? Stephanie looked around but couldn't see anything else apart from Mary's bag. That led Stephanie to wonder what Mary had to tell her. Would it be in her bag? It gaped open as it lay on the floor. She stepped towards it and peered inside without touching it. It looked nearly empty. No papers or photos visible. Stephanie wondered if her phone might be in there when people started to enter the room.

People in uniforms gently moved Stephanie

backwards and out of the room. A policewoman sat next to her and kindly asked Stephanie what had happened. Stephanie showed her Mary's text message and that she didn't know why Mary wanted to meet. The policewoman asked Stephanie to forward her the text as evidence.

"Are you sure you can't think why?"

"Not really. I knew she had found out that John Barry owned land plots in the village but I think it was something else."

"Did she email you anything?" The policewoman asked.

"I don't know. I'll look."

With shaking hands, Stephanie looked at her emails. There was something from Mary! She'd sent it at 7am. Both women eagerly looked at the photo in front of them.

"A barn?" Stephanie was confused.

"Where is that?"

Stephanie looked at the policewoman and shook her head slowly.

"I don't know what it means, or where it is," she replied. Her head throbbed and suddenly she felt exhausted.

"Click on the information," she pointed where to click and Stephanie touched the icon, but it just located it as being in Hibaldton. Stephanie sent her the image.

"Is there anyone who you can ring?"

Stephanie tried to think clearly as she was handed a hot cup of tea. Shivering she thought about what had happened. She remembered seeing Mark's car. She could ring Mark. What was he doing back? She could ring Lisa. She might be looking after her kids. What about mum and dad? They'd be worried.

She held the phone and rang Mark.

"Mark? Where are you, it's awful, something awful has happened." Stephanie trembled.

"Stephanie? Are you alright?" Mark sounded alarmed.

"I…I'm at the village hall. It's Mary. There's been an accident. The police are here."

"I'll be right there."

#

Mark entered the room. As soon as Stephanie saw him, she ran to him and burst into tears. He wrapped his arms around her and held her tight and before long they were free to go.

"What about Mary's husband?" Stephanie suddenly asked.

"Don't worry, Mr Grayling and the police are going round to talk with him. Go home and rest," the policewoman insisted.

As they slowly walked into the carpark, they

passed Bryan Grayling talking to a policeman with Frank, the caretaker. There was an ambulance and three police cars in the carpark. One policeman was standing at the exit, he let them drive out onto the road. Stephanie looked back at the scene and felt numb.

#

"You're in shock Steph, here have this. Just take sips."

Mark handed her a glass. Stephanie did as he said, and the drink felt warm as it slid down her throat and tingled her mouth.

"Luckily I found some brandy in your cupboard."

"Dad bought it for me at Christmas."

They sat on the settee in silence for a while until Stephanie felt like talking.

"I don't understand how she could have fallen. Maybe she was pushed!" Stephanie whispered aghast. "She could have entered the building with someone before I got there-I was a bit late."

"Why would anyone want to hurt her?"

"Maybe they didn't mean to…maybe they had an argument. Do you think it could have been John Barry?"

"I don't know… he does have a mean streak.

I remember when he argued with my dad once. It was when we were in sixth form. I heard shouting outside the house, so I ran to the door. I was just in time to see John push my dad on the shoulder. It was hard enough to knock him backward. If I hadn't had held my dad back. he would have punched him!" Mark grimaced at the memory.

"What were they arguing about?"

"Oh, he'd been pressuring my family to sell him some of our land by the river. He got angry because my dad said he didn't care how much money he offered, he'd never sell our land- especially to him…. And I remember that John said that he couldn't stop him."

Stephanie sat up. She counted on her fingers:

"One- Mary had found out that he was buying up land to build houses on. Two- She told Mr Grayling about it. John could have found out. Three- He'd been trying to get you to sell your land."

"Who else did Mary arrange to meet?" Mark asked.

"She didn't say…but she sent me this."

Stephanie showed Mark the photo of the barn and they both looked at it. "It looks familiar but it's difficult to tell as it was taken at night."

"It could be any farmer's barn," Mark

shrugged.

"What if it's on John's land. Ooh, what if it's the one by the river? Mary did go for a walk to the river…"

Mark seemed to be thinking hard.

Stephanie stood up. She didn't know if it was the brandy but she was feeling determined to get to the bottom of Mary's death. Deep inside she had a bad feeling. She knew it wasn't an accident. She started to pace up and down. "We should go see Mary's husband, maybe he knows something."

"I don't think now is the time to bother him, Stephanie."

There was a sharp knock at the door and in walked Lisa. She ran over to Stephanie and flung her arms around her. "Oh my god Stephanie, I came right over when I heard. I can stay with you today if you want. It must have been awful!"

Mark stood up. "I can see you're in good hands. I'll go…I've got things I've got to do."

"You're leaving?" Stephanie didn't want him to go. "She couldn't believe that he was going after what had just happened.

Mark held Stephanie's hand in his, "You need to have a lie down Steph and I know Lisa will look after you. I need to finish something, but if you're feeling ok tomorrow will you come to my house? I'll cook us something."

"Ok," She watched him go and sat down on the settee next to Lisa.

"What happened?" Lisa asked

Stephanie shook her head attempting to erase the image of Mary's blood stained face from her memory.

"I...I don't understand what , why?" Stephanie began with difficulty.

Lisa held Stephanie's hand gently.

"Tell me why you went to the village hall in the first place."

Stephanie showed Lisa the message on her phone and the photo of the barn. She described the scene in the meeting room and how the caretaker tried his best to save Mary's life.

"It looked like she hit her head on the table...but I don't know how it could have happened, the only thing I could see on the floor was her bag."

"Maybe she tripped over that?" Lisa wondered. "Was it open?"

"Yes, it was wide open. I could see inside but couldn't see anything unusual. I didn't really look properly. Damn, I should have searched the pockets before the police got there."

"You couldn't do that." Lisa sounded shocked, "Your fingerprints would have been all over it and the police would have thought it was you that killed her."

"Why would I want to do that?" Stephanie looked at Lisa in horror.

"Why would anyone want to kill poor Mary?" Lisa shrugged.

They sat in silence for a while.

"Pour me another brandy will you and have some yourself."

Stephanie finished off her drink and held out the glass to Lisa with trembling hands.

The two girls talked some more and then Stephanie decided to go have a lie down.

In the evening, Lisa ordered pizza and they watched a movie to try to take their minds off the events of the day. Stephanie's mum rang when she heard the news. She heard from Bev about Mary and wanted to know if Stephanie needed her to go round, but she told her mum that Lisa was there, and not to worry.

7
THE INVESTIGATION BEGINS

As Stephanie walked into the kitchen, she could hear the kettle boiling. Lisa had stayed the night and was at the breakfast bar spreading jam on some toast.

"Morning Stephanie, how are you?"

"Oh I'm ok, I think. I just can't believe yesterday happened!"

"I know," Lisa replied handing her the toast.

Stephanie took a grateful bite and watched her friend make the tea.

"Will you come with me to see Mary's husband?"

"Do you think he'll know anything?"

"Mary must have said something. I need to know what the photo of the barn was about. I just can't stop thinking about it. I was thinking we could go round with a pie or something. That's what they do in the movies don't they."

"Have you got a pie?"

"There's some in the freezer."

"You can't take a frozen pie!" Lisa looked appalled. "What type is it?"

" Chicken pie."

"Well, that's alright then." Lisa laughed.

"Really?"

"No! … How about if we make something like a shepherd's pie, that's easy."

"I've got some frozen mince."

"Well, that will be cottage pie then," Lisa explained.

"Oh, I can never remember which is which."

"You don't often see shepherds looking after cows, do you?" Lisa laughed.

"Oh yeah," Stephanie realised. "What do you call farmers who look after cows?"

"I don't know, oh I've just realised why they're called shepherds. They herd sheep."

"So people who herd cows must be cowherds…oh…"

"Cowards! Ha-ha." They both laughed.

It felt wrong to laugh though, so soon after Mary's passing. They continued to make the pie almost in silence. It had become therapy and an offering to Mary's husband to show their respect.

Walking along the road with her mum's

casserole dish in her hands, Lisa felt silly. She was wearing Stephanie's oven gloves because the dish was still hot.

"Hey, why am I carrying this dish, it was your idea!" Lisa moaned.

"Oh sorry," Stephanie said as she tried to take it from Lisa. It was difficult transferring oven gloves from one hand to the other.

"I told you a frozen pie would have been better," Stephanie remarked.

"Morning," nodded an elderly couple walked past with their highland terrier. They eyed the casserole dish with annoyance as their dog started yapping at Stephanie's legs and it tried to jump up towards the smell.

" Err, morning," Stephanie tried to shake it off while the lady pulled at the lead. Stephanie turned around holding the dish up in the air but she ended up with the lead wrapped around her legs. In the end, the man picked up the dog, who was trying its best to lick Stephanie's oven gloves, and Lisa helped to unwind the lead.

"Sorry," Stephanie apologised, and they walked on leaving the two frazzled people to return their dog to normal.

"Actually, I don't know why I'm apologising," said Stephanie, "it wasn't our fault."

#

Stephanie and Lisa stood at the door to Mary's house. It was easy to know which house it was because it had a bright, yellow door. It was in a row of quaint cottages behind the church. There was no sign of anyone around. They knocked and waited. No response. The front of the house was on an old narrow road, so Lisa could easily peer through the window to see if anyone was in. She shook her head, so they entered the narrow alley between the houses to see if there was anyone at the back. There was a little gate leading to the back garden. It was open so they walked through.

Lisa approached the back window and called, "I can see him. He's sat in his chair."

She knocked lightly on the window to get his attention. "Hellooo. Are you ok?" she shouted through the glass.

Stephanie waited and watched as Lisa put her hands up to the window. She then slowly turned to Stephanie, her face as white as a ghost.

"I think you should ring the police."

"Why?"

Stephanie put her face up to the window. Mary's husband was sitting still, staring ahead. His eyes never twitched; his face was frozen.

"Oh God, not again."

The two women stared at each other in

shock.

Lisa looked again into the room.

"Can you see any sign of a struggle?" Stephanie asked.

She also peered in. Everything looked in place. There was a coffee table with one empty glass and next to it, a bottle of whiskey half empty.

"It looks like he was drowning his sorrows," Lisa noted.

"Look, under his chair!" Stephanie gasped.

Laying open and empty was what looked like a pill bottle.

"Do you think he's still alive? We should break in!" Stephanie lifted the dish up to the glass.

"Try the door first!" Lisa screamed and held her arm back.

They ran around and Lisa tried the handle. It opened. They ran in and Stephanie plonked the casserole dish on the coffee table while Lisa shook Mary's husband vigorously.

"Aargh!" they cried and jumped back as he fell sideways.

He was as stiff as a board.

"I think he's been dead a while." Lisa whispered.

They backed out of the room as if in rewind.

Stephanie even picked up her dish then they went back outside panting heavily.

#

After talking to the police, the two young women returned to the front of the house which now had two police cars and an ambulance outside. All the neighbours had come out to watch. Mrs Moore was standing outside her house talking to a policeman and Stephanie saw her look up and point at them.

"Great. Now everyone's going to think that I had something to do with these deaths," Stephanie groaned.

"Come on, let's see what she's saying." Lisa pulled Stephanie across the road, still clutching the casserole dish. They were just in time to hear the policeman thank her and return across the road. He'd already spoken to Stephanie and Lisa, but he still looked at them suspiciously as he left.

"Oh this is just awful, just awful." Mrs Moore shook her head. "But they do say that you can die of a broken heart. The poor man was devastated when his wife died. I heard that it's very common for one spouse to die soon after the death of the other"

"But not the next day!" Lisa reacted.

"Or that night....we don't know when it

happened do we?" Stephanie stated clearly, eyes wide. "We just found him like that. We absolutely did not have anything to do with it. Did we Lisa?"

Mrs Moore looked from Stephanie to Lisa. Lisa stared at Stephanie as if she was crazy.

Lisa stood in front of Stephanie, giving her a chance to calm down.

Stephanie took off one of the oven gloves and lifted off the dish lid. She scooped a bit of mash potato and ate it. She was feeling nervous, and it gave her something to do. Actually, it tasted really good, so she went in for a deeper scoop.

"Did you see anything suspicious Mrs Moore?" Lisa asked.

"Do you think that I spend my day looking out of my window?" the old woman looked offended.

Stephanie and Lisa just looked at her in silence.

"Well, as it happens, I was looking out quite a bit to see if I could find out who's been leaving dog mess outside my drive."

"And?" Lisa waited impatiently.

"I still don't know who's doing it."

"But did you see anyone going into his house?"

"Oh, there were lots of people yesterday, you know paying their respects. I saw Mr Grayling go in with the police. The policeman left but Mr Grayling stayed for longer. What a lovely man he is…so…commanding," Mrs Moore smiled to herself.

"What do you mean?"

"Well …he takes control of the situation doesn't he. He looked after him as he didn't feel like talking to anyone. Well, you wouldn't feel like seeing people when your wife had just …parted like that. I went to pay my respects you see, and he never said a word. Poor soul." She nodded over to the house.

"Who else did you see?"

"Erm… I saw Trevor Cook, from the shop, visit- he brought a bottle of whiskey and he didn't stay long. The Reverend stayed for a while, I'm sure he was a great comfort. Mary and Gordon didn't have any children. Mary's sister is in Australia and Gordon's brother died a few years ago so I don't know who to contact here. That's what I told the police and Mr Grayling when he asked."

"Was there anything out of the ordinary?"

Stephanie was disappointed.

"Not really. There was a brown sporty car I'd not seen before. It was parked on the road for a while, but I was making a cup of hot milk, and when I came back it was gone."

"Was that while Mr Grayling was there? Did you see who it belonged to?" Stephanie asked urgently.

"Ooh let me see. It was about 8 o'clock, I think. That looks nice by the way, is it a casserole?" Mrs Moore raised her drawn on eyebrows and nodded at the dish.

Stephanie had her mouth full and swallowed quickly,

"Oh its Shepherd's pie,"

Lisa stared at her friend and shook her head slowly.

"Well, I get hungry when I'm stressed!" Stephanie explained.

"Cottage pie," Lisa corrected her.

"Cottage pie." Stephanie sighed. "You can have it if you like Mrs Moore." Stephanie said reluctantly.

"Oh really? Thank you."

Mrs Moore took the dish. Stephanie was surprised, she didn't think she'd say yes!

"So?" Stephanie asked again getting exasperated by now.

"Hmm?"

Mrs Moore had forgotten what they were talking about.

"Was Mr Grayling still there when you saw the car?" Stephanie reminded her.

"I don't think Mr Grayling would have been there by then. I didn't see who owned the car. Maybe it was a relative after all."

This conversation had reached a dead end, literally. Stephanie and Lisa thanked her and walked away. They walked down the road back towards Stephanie's house. Stephanie was thinking who the car could have belonged to. The police probably tracked down a relative. It was annoying that she was no closer to finding out about the barn, and now it was getting very serious. Two deaths in the village. What was going on? Did Mary's husband take an overdose? Did someone give it to him?

"The expression on his face wasn't very peaceful, was it?"

"I was just thinking that."

Lisa could still see Gordon's face in her mind.

"He looked shocked; it was horrible. I remember when my uncle died in his sleep, and he didn't look like that." Lisa shivered.

Stephanie linked her oven gloved hand through Lisa's arm,

"I'm glad you were with me." she told her. "Let's go back and plan our next step."

#

Stephanie and Lisa spent a couple of hours discussing everything they knew so far, and Stephanie got out a notepad to record it.

'Mary and Gordon- accident or murder?

Suspects…'

They concluded that everyone at the Parish Council meeting should be a suspect. Mary had been taking notes about the housing development. She had seen more traffic by the river. Everyone at the pub was a suspect too. Who had overheard Mary talking to Stephanie about her suspicions? John Barry was prime suspect. Reverend Pierce? No, she crossed his name out. Mr Cook? He gave Gordon the whiskey. Who owned the brown sports car? Bryan Grayling- who was he talking to in the pub?

"We should go see John Barry and see if he owns the barn in the photo," Stephanie said as she underlined 'prime suspect' twice.

"He's not likely to admit anything," Lisa said.

"I'd still like to see his reaction. Shall we go to see him now?"

"What about your date with Mark. Shouldn't you be getting ready?"

"Oh gosh, I forgot! I don't even know what time."

Lisa said she had to go home anyway and told

Stephanie not to do anything without her. Then she had to make it clear she meant with John Barry…not with Mark Proctor! Stephanie should do anything she wished with Mark! Stephanie pretended to push her out the door. It was good to laugh after all the tension of the day.

8
EVERYONE IS A SUSPECT

Stephanie looked at the clock. It was nearly 3pm. She should have a bite to eat and then get ready for tonight. She'd been so busy; she hadn't had time to feel nervous about going to Mark's house. She couldn't wait to see inside the place. Maybe she was a natural investigator. She certainly was nosy enough she had to admit.

As she made a quick sandwich, she looked across the field at Mark's house and wondered what kind of home he would have. He did say that he hadn't had a chance to buy lots of furniture. Maybe it would still be quite bare, with boxes still to be unpacked. Stephanie ran a bath as she wondered what to wear. Should she go for sexy? She looked in her wardrobe. She didn't really have anything sexy, and she didn't want to make it obvious. She owned a little black dress, a skirt….. Stephanie felt the skirt, it was silky smooth. She always felt good wearing it, and she could match it with a short top with thin straps. She could wear it with a little woollen cardigan. Sorted. Now for that relaxing bath. Just what she needed!

While she was straightening her hair, her phone pinged- a text.

Stephanie picked it up to see that Mark had asked if he could pick her up at 6. She thought about how to reply. She didn't want to sound too eager. "That's fine. See you soon." She texted.

She looked at the clock and saw she had one more hour. She had plenty of time to finish getting dressed and put on some makeup. She never wore too much make up, just enough to even out her skin tone. She brushed on some blusher and eye shadow, choosing brown to match her eyes. Stephanie looked in her jewellery box and picked out a silver necklace with a small bee pendant. It was tricky fastening it behind her neck as her hands were shaking a little. She'd thought about what to take with her. She popped some toiletries into a bag with some clean underwear, a warmer top and some leggings. Well, she wanted to be prepared! He didn't need to know what was in there and she might stay in the spare room....or not.

"I need a glass of wine," she decided and went downstairs into the kitchen.

She was just finishing her glass when she saw a car pull up. She went to the door.

"Hi," Stephanie smiled.

"Hi back," Mark grinned. He followed her into the kitchen as she picked up her bag. As she stood ready, she watched him pick up her notepad that was lying on the breakfast bar.

"What's this Miss Marple?" he teased.

"Lisa and I were just making notes," Stephanie tried to get it back, but he held it in the air.

"Mary and Gordon- accident or murder? Suspects…"

"So everyone at the parish council is a suspect?" Mark asked turning his back on Stephanie so he could read more. Then he stopped, staring at the pad. "Mary and Gordon?" he said quickly and gave the book back. "What do you mean by that?"

"Didn't you know? …. Lisa and I went to visit Mary's husband today and…" Stephanie could see that Mark looked shocked.

"And?"

"He was dead in his chair. There was a half empty bottle of whiskey and an empty bottle of sleeping pills under his chair."

Mark put his hand through his hair, and he walked into the front room.

"Why didn't you tell me you were going to see him?" Mark demanded.

He sounded annoyed.

"I didn't know, it was a last-minute decision. Then it all happened so fast. I had Lisa with me, so we came home to think."

"I don't want you to investigate this anymore Steph."

"Why not? Don't you think we owe it to Mary and Gordon? We can't just forget about it."

"I'm not saying that we forget about it. Look, I've been doing some investigating myself. I didn't want you to get involved because it could be dangerous."

"Well tell me what you know."

Stephanie folded her arms in defiance. So, it was ok for him to investigate but not her!

"Don't look at me like that Steph."

He walked closer and put his hands on her shoulders.

"You look very sexy when you're mad."

Stephanie's face felt hot, and she tried to be annoyed but he was standing so close. She couldn't think so she stepped back. Her chin tilted up to him.

"Just tell me what you're going to do next."

He breathed deeply, "For a start…I'm going to take you back to my house."

He took her hand and they walked to the door.

"Wait, my bag!" Stephanie grabbed the bag and her keys.

He opened the door of his car for her, and she slipped down into the low seat. As the car pulled away Stephanie was determined not to let him evade the question.

"What did you mean when you said you'd been investigating?"

"Basically, I'm in contact with a detective from Scotland Yard. They're looking into it. I'll ring him tomorrow to make sure they have connected Gordon's death with Mary's."

"Is there something you're not telling me?" Stephanie looked at him in the twilight. She could see the silhouette of his face as he concentrated on driving down the bumpy lane past his parent's farm.

"Of course not. If I hear anything, I'll let you know. You know how the police are…they don't share what they know. But he did say that there is something going on and it's dangerous. There. So, stop asking questions Stephanie. I don't want you to get hurt."

It was a relief to hear that the police were

taking it seriously. Stephanie waited while Mark walked round the car to open her door. He was being very attentive, and she might as well enjoy it. The last few days had been hell, it would be nice to relax and forget everything for one night.

9
A NIGHT TO REMEMBER

They arrived at Mark's house. Stephanie had been dying to see inside. She stepped though a wooden porch and then through to a huge open space. "Wow!" she breathed as she walked in looking around her. It was amazing! Against the wall was a wide-open fireplace with a real fire burning in the grate. The mantel piece was made of a thick piece of timber, and she looked up to see a high beamed ceiling. She could see upstairs as there was a balcony revealing a landing and doors which probably led to bedrooms. The staircase was on her left, and at the other side of the stairs was another corridor.

"Let me show you round," Mark said proudly.

He led Stephanie around the stairs to show her a study, a downstairs toilet, and a utility room. Next, Stephanie found herself at the back of the house. There was a dining table in front of a row of bifold doors. She couldn't see outside as it was black but twinkly lights hung above the doors and along the wall. Stephanie walked, entranced, into the kitchen and full circle, back into the main room.

"Its…gorgeous Mark! I wasn't expecting this. Did you design this yourself?"

"With help from my friend. He's an architect in London. It was his idea to have a balcony so you can see down into the living room. This enables me to have this huge open space, and the heat from the fire rises to fill the house. Do you like it?" Mark looked at her with interest.

"Of course I do!" she laughed, twirling around. "What's not to like. I love it!"

Mark grinned at her. "What would you like to drink? Wine?"

He walked up to the kitchen and poured a glass of red wine that was standing on the work top. Stephanie noticed the dark leather settee and chairs and the cream rug in front of the fire. She was surprised it looked so homely.

"I thought you hadn't had chance to move in properly."

"Since then, I've had some deliveries," he smiled. "I wanted it to look nice before you came. When I was in London, I picked up some more personal things."

Stephanie was standing next to a bar stool, so she decided to climb onto it. It was easier said than done. She put the glass down, put her foot onto the metal rung and tried to hop up. Mark laughed and put his hands on either side of her waist to lift her up. When she was on the stool, he didn't make any attempt to move away. Stephanie could feel the warmth of his body close to hers and the heat of his hands as they slid down her waist to her thighs. His thumb stroked the skirt on her leg.

"I like this skirt," Mark said softly.

"It's my favourite," Stephanie managed to reply.

All she could think of was his hand was so close to the edge of her skirt, and how she wanted him to put his hand underneath. Stephanie held her breath waiting to see what he would do next.

Mark stepped back, looking flustered. He walked round the island and asked if Stephanie was hungry.

"What have you made?" Stephanie finally managed to say.

She looked towards the source of the delicious smell and saw a large, black and metal slow cooker.

"Lamb casserole. I hope you like it."

"Ha-ha, shepherd's pie or cottage pie?" Stephanie laughed.

Then she realised that he wouldn't understand the joke.

"I can never remember which is which, can you?" Mark remarked.

"Exactly! It smells lovely! Do you like to cook?"

"I dabble…. but I haven't really had the time or the kitchen to do it justice. Do you like lamb?" he asked, worried.

"Oh yes," said Stephanie.

"Shall we sit at the table?" Mark asked.

Stephanie stepped down from the stool and carried her glass across to the dining table. Mark pulled back the chair for her to sit down.

Stephanie sipped her wine and enjoyed watching Mark move around his kitchen. He was wearing blue jeans with a dark blue shirt. The shirt was casually untucked, and he had rolled the sleeves slightly up to reveal his strong forearms. They both had taken off their shoes when they entered, and the sight of Mark walking about in socks, looking so relaxed, made Stephanie smile. It all felt so perfect, so right. Soft music drifted across from the front room and the fairy lights glowed a dark yellow.

"Bon Appetit." Mark said as he placed two

dishes on the table.

He then brought over a large bowl filled with pieces of fresh bread.

"Cheers." Stephanie raised her glass and Mark did the same.

" Cheers. I think you need a refill." Mark noticed and brought over the bottle.

"Not too much, I already had a glass before you picked me up."

"Oh yeah?" Mark laughed, "I'll have to catch up then."

He finished his glass and poured another.

"I guess I was a little nervous about tonight," Stephanie admitted.

"Me too," Mark replied, "I've been busy today, so I got up early to make dinner. I was chopping vegetables at 6 this morning."

"Oh my goodness!" Stephanie suddenly cried out.

"What?" Mark dropped his spoon in surprise.

"I completely forgot! I never asked you how you got on with your meeting. Was it successful?"

Mark laughed and clutched his chest.

"Oh God, I thought there was something in the casserole like an eye or something."

"Well if there was an eye, you definitely would have known about it. Jeez."

"Ha-ha. The meeting went very well, they seemed excited about taking us on, but we won't find out for a few days. I was going to stay, but I just wanted to come home- to see you."

Stephanie reached for some bread and dipped it into her casserole. They were both quiet for a while as they ate. It tasted delicious and Stephanie felt like she needed to eat something to soak up the wine she'd had.

"This is delicious," Stephanie said with her mouth full.

She looked around her.

"This is a great space for entertaining."

"I've not been the one for dinner parties in the past, but I can imagine doing it here."

"Didn't any of your girlfriends cook?"

Mark smiled and looked a bit embarrassed. " Err I have not really had a serious enough relationship like that."

When Stephanie raised her eyebrows he continued, "I admit that when I went to Uni, I probably lived quite a wild lifestyle. I partied a lot, stayed up late, you know worked hard played hard. When I got a job… that sort of continued really." He shrugged. "I'm fed up with that life. I had a look in the mirror and decided that I needed to make a change. It was about then when my mum rang me up and said dad needed my help. So here I am."

"I'm glad you did." Stephanie reached out her hand and touched his. Their fingers entwined and Stephanie looked from their hands to Mark's face. The glow from the lights danced in his eyes. The top of his shirt was unbuttoned just enough to see his throat and Stephanie wanted to touch his chest and kiss his neck. She imagined him kissing her and the thrill made her pull her hand back. Stephanie's face flushed and she looked down for her napkin nervously.

"Did I tell you how lovely you look?" Mark spoke quietly as if he didn't want to spoil the energy that surrounded them.

Stephanie looked up and could see that his face looked flushed too. She smiled, "You don't look so bad yourself."

"Not so bad?" he pretended to sound offended.

Stephanie thought his smile was very sexy. He had a cute dimple in his cheek and his chin had a little stubble which suited him. Mark definitely looked hot, but Stephanie was too embarrassed to say that anyway, she had a feeling he knew it.

Mark stood up and walked around the table. Taking her hands, he pulled her gently up to him.

They both stood barely touching, reading

each other's body language. There was no doubt what was in their thoughts. Stephanie's mouth reached up to be kissed and Mark held her close, their mouths found each other hungrily. Mark's shirt felt smooth and hot under her touch. Stephanie could feel his heart beating and she closed her eyes as his lips brushed her neck and his hands gently pushed her cardigan from off her shoulders. He kissed her shoulders as his hands reached up under her top following her spine and down round her waist. She arched her back in exquisite pleasure, she leant against his legs feeling how hard he was against her body.

Mark whispered against her ear. "Steph, I've wanted to do this for so long."

They both stepped back until Stephanie was against the table edge.

"You haven't given me the full tour of the house yet," she breathed huskily.

Mark held her hand and led her upstairs.

The first room they came to he stopped.

"Are you sure you want to see my room, because if you come in, I can't promise I'll be gentle."

Stephanie walked him backwards into the room and lifted his shirt over his head. His shoulders were broad and so sexy! Her breathing quickened as he turned them round so her back was against the open door. He lifted her arms and held her hands together as he bent to kiss her mouth, chin, neck. His other hand took down a strap off her shoulder, then the other. His tongue licked across the top of her breast, his hands pulling down her top to reveal her full breasts aching with desire underneath her lacy bra. Mark lifted her up, so her legs encircled his hips and he carried her over to the bed. Stephanie watched as he took down his trousers and boxers. She quickly slipped out of her top and skirt.

"I need a condom," he muttered, reaching into the drawer. She watched him put it on then she lay back. Mark took a long look at Stephanie, from her head down to her toes. She pulled down her underwear, then passion took over. Their kisses were fast and powerful. Stephanie pushed herself eagerly against him, she couldn't wait any longer. Aroused and wet, she could feel the orgasm building up inside her. She cried out as his hands cupped her bottom and lifted her to him. Her bent knees lifted higher for him to enter as deep as he could. Their bodies moved together as one until they both reached extasy and then they parted, lying next to each other flushed and breathless. They lay together with legs entwined. Stephanie felt hot and her body purred with pleasure. Her face was on Mark's chest, and she listened to his heart beating rapidly, waiting for it to return to normal.

Stephanie got up to go to the ensuite. When she returned, he had got under the covers and was sitting with a huge smile on his face. He lifted back the sheet for her to snuggle next to him.

"I warned you I might not be gentle." He breathed into her ear as he started to kiss her again.

"Do you see me complaining?" Stephanie replied.

Mark laughed, "You are so beautiful Steph. That was the teenager in me, wanting you so desperately. And now, the man in me wants to know every part of your body…This time we'll take it slow….."

#

It was late in the evening, when they ventured downstairs again. Mark replenished the dying fire as Stephanie curled up on the settee. Mark had given her his dressing gown, and he had slipped into some jogging pants and a white t-shirt. He handed her a bowl of ice-cream and they sat eating while chatting about memories from school.

"I had a big crush on you, you know," Steph laughed.

"I knew there was something between us. Do you remember when I was playing football and I was so busy looking over at you that the ball hit me in the face?" Mark held his nose as if reliving the moment. "There was blood everywhere!"

Stephanie gasped as she recalled. "I remember! I didn't know you were looking at me."

"Yes! I also noticed that you were the only one who didn't laugh at me. You looked shocked and upset. That meant a lot."

"I wanted to rush over and see if you were ok, but I didn't really know you. If you liked me, why didn't you ask me out?"

Mark thought about it. "I was stupid, and it wasn't the right time. I was nearly finished at sixth form, I was going to Uni… "

His voice trailed off. "I kept in touch with Stan, Amy's brother. She was in your year, and he kept me in the loop about most people. I heard that you'd gone to teaching college. When I came back, I hoped you'd not gone far away."

Stephanie thought about what he had said. She did feel that there was something between them at sixth form. Every time they passed each other, she had felt like she might faint, and he did watch her as she went by. But not asking her out had made her feel so empty. She missed him so much when he wasn't there anymore.

"I'm really sorry," Mark said as he kissed her gently and held her close. "Like I said, I was really stupid!"

After a while he asked, "So what shall we do tomorrow?"

"Aren't you at work?"

"Nope. I thought we could do something together. What do you fancy doing? We could just stay in bed all day, I don't mind."

Stephanie poked him in the ribs and laughed. "I bet you don't! We could go for a walk, or do some shopping? Is there anything you still need?"

"Well, what do you think?"

Stephanie stood up and looked around. "You could do with some cushions."

Mark laughed, "Typical female response."

"No! Cushions can give a pop of colour to the room actually. Plus, you can change the covers to fit the mood or season."

"Season?"

"You know like Christmas. Oh, your room will be so amazing at Christmas. You could fit a huge Christmas tree in the corner over there!"

Stephanie started to get excited at the scene in her mind.

Mark looked and grinned, "I can't believe you're planning Christmas already. But I'm happy that you are. Ok cushion shopping tomorrow then."

"Ok, but we can still have a lie in……" Stephanie smiled and reached for his hand to take him back to bed.

10
THE DAY AFTER

Around mid-day, after a shower, Stephanie was finishing her tour of upstairs while Mark was in the bathroom. She was wearing leggings and a long t-shirt that she'd brought with her, she was glad that she had. Stephanie walked onto the landing and looked over the balcony down into the living room. The embers in the fireplace were grey, and the curtains were closed. The room wasn't in darkness though, as the sun shone through the doors and window from the kitchen.

Stephanie turned and walked to the next room. She opened the door to find a spare room. The room was empty apart from fitted wardrobes. She walked across the room to the window. It overlooked the runway of the local airfield. Recently, the planes had started to circle round, getting ready for the new season of parachute jumping. It was one of the reasons why Stephanie loved her house. She'd grown up playing at her grandma's, watching parachutes spiralling from the sky over the field behind her house. Stephanie searched the view for her house. She guessed where her house was along the line of homes, picking out the tree at the end of her garden.

Next, she looked in another room. This was also a spare room, again empty. Wow, was there even a spare bed for her to stay in if she hadn't have slept with Mark? She looked out at the view from this angle. Behind his house, there was a garden area and behind that a field. In that field was a barn and a track went from the road, past the barn and up the edge of the field. A man was down below getting into a van.

"That's Dave," Mark's voice behind her made her jump. "He'll be moving some stuff about. Come on, let's go then."

Mark put his arm around her waist, and he gave it a little squeeze that sent goosebumps up her body.

#

They drove down the motorway to Leeds, and Stephanie introduced Mark to Ikea. He couldn't believe that there could be so much stuff in one place. They left with a huge bag of all sorts of things for the house: candles, plants, squeegee, vase…. everything but a cuddly toy. Stephanie had to stop him from buying her one.

Next, they visited Habitat, where they chose some cushions, and Mark chose deep red. He also spotted a coffee table he liked and ordered that to be delivered. Stephanie reminded him that he needed to buy beds for the spare rooms.

"Yes, er… I suppose you are wondering where I expected you to sleep," Mark looked sheepishly at Stephanie.

"I did wonder."

Stephanie looked at Mark and raised her eyebrows teasing him.

"Ok, I admit I did hope that you would sleep with me in my room…"

Stephanie pretended to gasp as if she had no idea.

"…but if you didn't, I would have slept on the settee or rung for a taxi."

Stephanie laughed and put her arm through his as they walked back to the car.

They finished off the day with a meal at the nearby restaurant. Pizza followed by hot chocolate fudge cake. Stephanie definitely needed to go jogging again!

When they got back to Hibaldton, Stephanie

thought about going home.

"I do want to come back with you, but I need a change of clothes and I've got work to do," Stephanie groaned.

"It's Saturday tomorrow. You can grab some clothes and I'll take you home on Sunday. Don't you want to help me place my cushions? What about all that other stuff that needs a home? Hell, I don't even remember what I've bought!"

"That's the magic of Ikea," Stephanie laughed. "Ok you win."

They stopped off at Stephanie's so she could pack some clean clothes, then they headed back to Mark's house.

As the car approached the entrance to his drive, Mark slowed down as they noticed a white Porsche parked in front of his house. Stephanie looked at Mark and saw his eyes narrow and his lips pressed together.

"Fuck," he said under his breath. He stopped the car and started to reverse.

"What's wrong?" Stephanie asked, surprised by his reaction.

"There's someone I don't want to see."

The car door opened, and out stepped long legs covered in black boots up to the thigh. A tall young woman jumped out and raced over to them, arms waving in the air.

Mark was still determined to drive off, but Stephanie stopped him.

"Stop! You can't leave like that!" Stephanie cried out.

"Watch me," he replied.

Stephanie grabbed his arm. "Who is she?" she demanded.

Mark stepped on the brakes and looked at Stephanie.

"She's someone I know from London."

There was a pause like he was choosing his words carefully.

"There's nothing between us, honestly. She's just someone from a group of people I know."

Stephanie frowned. "So why don't you want me to meet her?"

"Cos she's crackers. It's not that I don't want you to meet her, It's that I don't want to see her right now."

He sighed and turned the car around to drive back. Standing next to the open car, she didn't look happy especially when she saw Stephanie. Her eyes stared at them like daggers. If looks could kill!

Mark grabbed Stephanie's arm, "Don't believe anything she says, it's all an act!" he warned, and then got out of the car.

Stephanie watched her run up to Mark and

throw her arms around him. Stephanie slowly got out of the car and walked towards them. She could see that Mark was looking very uncomfortable and the other woman was standing as close to him as she could. Or maybe Stephanie was the other woman….

Mark stepped away over to Stephanie.

"This is Kate. Kate, Steph."

"So pleased to meet you Steph. Any friend of Mark's is a friend of mine." She stepped towards Stephanie with her arms out and gave her one of those air kisses on either side of her face pulling her towards her at the same time as pushing her away. Stephanie had only seen people do that on telly so she just stood there looking at Mark.

"I was just telling Mark off for running away like that. He didn't tell me he was staying up here! I was expecting you to call me darling." She walked over to him and put her arm through his. "Come on now, show me this adorable house of yours."

They walked a few paces towards the door before Mark unravelled his arm and stopped.

"Hang on Kate. You can't just show up like this unannounced. How did you even know where I live?"

Kate pursed her lips and put on a show of looking hurt. "Oh I spoke to the gang and Paul and Angie gave me your parent's number. Your mother is adorable by the way. We get on so well you know," She aimed this last remark at Stephanie.

Mark looked like he was planning what to do next. Stephanie thought about leaving, but decided she was interested to see how this was going to play out. She imagined her Grandma Bettie here and thought this was just up her street.

"You must be tired from your drive Kate, why don't we go inside?" Stephanie motioned for Mark to open the door.

Mark took a deep breath and unlocked the door and they all walked inside.

Kate was the first to walk inside and Mark followed Stephanie.

Stephanie decided to make them a cup of tea, showing that she knew her way around the kitchen. Standing behind the kitchen island, she could also observe Kate and decide what to do.

Kate certainly had the air of a model about her. She also looked like she had money and was used to being waited on. Kate turned her back to Mark, expecting him to take her coat off. He looked over to Stephanie nervously while slipping her coat off and threw it over the back of the nearest settee. Kate was wearing a short black, leather skirt and a suit waist coat with no blouse underneath. A thick gold necklace shone around her neck. Stephanie did notice though that Mark didn't really pay attention to her body, probably for Stephanie's benefit. He walked into the kitchen with Stephanie and helped to make the tea.

Kate walked over to sit at the island. She was tall so had no trouble with the bar stool like Stephanie had done.

"I've missed you Markie baby," Kate sulked.

"We haven't seen each other for like 3 months!" Mark remarked impatiently.

"Well, I have been busy, so I thought I'd take some days off. I know I've been neglecting you darling."

"Kate, I've got a lot to do. I don't know why you're here but I'm sorry, I can't entertain you right now."

"But I was planning on staying for a few days. Stephanie can show me around if you're busy, can't you?"

Stephanie's mouth dropped in shock. Mark quickly said," Stephanie works so no she can't. You'd hate it here, there's nothing to do."

Kate put her elbow on the island top and perched her chin on her hand. She looked at Stephanie up and down.

"There must be a spa around here somewhere. My treat Stephanie, you look like you could do with a makeover." As Stephanie glared at her she defended herself, "Oh, don't take it the wrong way dear, but you are attractive, in… a country way…..and I can help!"

Stephanie looked at Mark with her mouth open, and Mark put his arms on Stephanie's shoulders as if he thought he'd have to hold her back.

"What Kate is trying to say, is that she likes to help people. It's her way that's all."

Stephanie had had enough of this drama and decided to go home.

"I'm sorry Kate, but I have some work I've got to do at home. Goodbye Mark, I'll see myself out."

She wriggled out of his arms and walked towards the door.

Mark followed her out and when they got on the drive, he reached to stop her.

"I'll drive you home Steph."

"I can walk, it's only there." She pointed across the field.

"Please! Let me drive you home and we can talk."

"We can talk another time; I fancy a walk

Mark. Bye."

Stephanie marched down the lane and left Mark standing there. She purposely didn't look back.

Stephanie didn't know what to think about all of that. She didn't want to listen to Mark at that moment because she knew she couldn't take it in. Last night and today had been bliss. It was too good to be true and it was better to find out now than later.

11
THE INVESTIGATION IS BACK ON

When Stephanie got home, she rang Lisa. Stephanie was angry at herself for nearly crying. She didn't regret spending the night with Mark. It was a night of passion which had been a long time coming, but she did regret that she'd been stupid enough to plan for the future with him. Lisa told her that she needed to take her mind off him, and their conversation inevitably led to the deaths of Mary and Gordon.

"Mark told me that he'd contacted a detective, but no one has been in touch. You'd have thought that he or she would want to talk to me or you, wouldn't you?"

"Maybe they will contact us next week," Lisa suggested.

"If they haven't by next week, then I think we should restart our own investigation. I think I should go see John Barry. We still don't know if he owns that barn in the photograph."

"That barn could be any barn in the area," Lisa remarked.

Stephanie remembered Mark had a similar barn behind his house. She thought about telling Lisa but decided not to."

"Did you see your email from Bryan?" Lisa remembered. "There's a Parish meeting this Wednesday to discuss Mary and Gordon's memorial service."

"Oh no, I haven't had chance to look. That gives us a chance to ask some questions," Stephanie got excited.

"I think you need to be careful Steph, don't make it obvious."

Stephanie agreed that she needed to think about how to approach it.

"The thing is, Bryan Grayling never talks to us. I need to think of a reason to get his attention."

"Oh, I've got to go," Lisa said urgently." The dog's got hold of my washing! See ya tomorrow!"

Stephanie laughed and hung up. Right, this investigation was just what she needed to focus her mind.

#

Sunday was spent at her parents' house as usual. As she approached the front door, she was met by what Stephanie could only describe as Ronald Macdonald if he'd turned into an 80-year-old woman. Grandma Bettie was on top form. She'd had her hair dyed bright orange and was wearing a frilly white blouse and checked trousers. All she need was a pair of long shoes and a big flower that squirted water and then Stephanie would be looking out for a tiny car parked outside.

"Hello Stephanie, I've been dying to get all the gossip. So, what's the news about Gordon?"

Grandma Bettie ushered Stephanie inside and looked around outside to make sure no one was watching.

"The word on the street is he died of a broken heart, but what do you think. Do you think he was bumped off?"

Barbara was in the kitchen setting the table.

"Oh, what nonsense, he wasn't bumped off," she said laughing.

"We don't live in a 70s movie Bettie." Malcolm called out from the front room. It's not Starsky and Hutch!"

Malcolm came into the kitchen and saw Bettie's hair.

"Oh God I forgot."

He looked quickly away and sat down at the table.

Barbara had started to make extra Yorkshire puddings to avoid arguments and they tucked into their beef Sunday lunch. Stephanie was vague when asked about Mark. Every time someone asked about him, she steered the conversation round to talk about Bettie's health. Soon her mum and dad got the hint.

Stephanie told them about the meeting to discuss the memorial service and that she'd let them know when it was to be held.

"I can't believe it was you who found Mary and Gordon like that," Barbara said looking concerned at her daughter. "Are you sure you're ok?"

"Yes, I'm fine," Stephanie said.

"Maybe, I should come and visit you," Grandma Bettie mentioned, "it sounds more exciting where you live."

"You have a spare room, don't you?" Malcolm sounded keen on the idea.

"Nonsense mum, all your friends are here and there isn't a regular bus service."

Barbara started to clear away the plates.

"Just be careful Stephanie."

"It's not like there's going to be any more dead bodies!" Stephanie told them.

"You never know…" Grandma said, "there could be a mass murderer living in your village."

"You mean a serial killer," Stephanie corrected her.

"Oh my goodness! Stop it!" Barbara demanded, putting her hands to her ears. "My daughter isn't going to live in a place with a serial murderer!"

"I'm not!" Stephanie sighed. "Look, I have to go. Don't worry!"

She kissed her mum goodbye, gave her grandma and dad a hug, and left for home.

#

Wednesday came quickly and the village meeting was that evening. Mark had obviously decided it was best to give Stephanie some space as he hadn't called or texted. She didn't know or care what had happened to Kate. Well, ok she did care but she tried not to think about it.

The meeting was arranged for 6 o'clock and Stephanie wasn't looking forward to seeing Mark again. She had stayed behind at school to mark some assessments, so she took the car to the Village Hall.

They all sat around the big table, much as they had done before. The mood was very sombre this time though. There was an empty chair next to Bryan where Mary had sat. Mrs Cook had agreed to take the minutes of the meeting for the time being. Mark sat across the table from Stephanie. He had come in when everyone was sitting down, so Stephanie hadn't noticed him until they were in their seats. She avoided his gaze and looked down the table towards the chairman.

"Good evening everyone," Mr Grayling began. "It is of course an extremely sad time and I wish we were meeting under different circumstances."

"Very sad, very sad indeed," Mrs Moore commented.

He coughed and stared down at his papers. "We are, of course, here to discuss the memorial service for our dear departed friends, Mary and Gordon. I hand you over to our vicar, Reverend Pierce for the details."

The reverend took over and gave the time and date for the service. He couldn't say when the funeral would be as the police had yet to release the bodies, but the service would be held that Sunday at 10 o'clock. The Parish would provide the flowers and Mrs Moore was going to order the wreath.

Stephanie thought that it was a positive sign that the police hadn't released the bodies. She had not heard from any detectives but surely this meant that they were still holding an investigation.

"Is there any news from the police about their investigation?" Stephanie asked.

Mr Grayling looked up and answered," Why should there be an investigation?"

Stephanie replied, "I thought that if they hadn't released their bodies, then it was because they were still investigating the circumstances of their deaths."

"I am sure that it is just a formality. The last thing our village needs is gossip."

"I wasn't…"Stephanie started but was interrupted by Bryan.

"I have been in close contact with the authorities, and there is absolutely nothing to investigate. They were both very tragic but accidental deaths. Gordon was extremely depressed when I saw him. Let us concentrate on celebrating the value they both meant to our community."

"Here, here," Mrs Moore said, and there were nods and agreements around the room.

It was a short meeting, but no one seemed in a rush to leave. Everyone mingled and discussed their memories. Stephanie was watching John Barry, she wanted to talk to him but didn't want everyone to see. He had been very quiet and seemed to be moving towards the door. Just when Stephanie was thinking about catching him outside, Bryan Grayling was standing opposite her.

"I understand that it was you Stephanie who found both Mary and Gordon. I'm very sorry that you had to go through that."

Stephanie looked up at him, he seemed genuinely upset for her.

"Yes, it was awful."

"But how was it that you were meeting with Mary in the first place?"

Stephanie thought about what to reveal. She knew that Mary had told Mr Grayling about all the land purchased by John Barry, but had she shown him the photo of the barn?

"Mary sent me a photo and she was going to talk to me about it."

"Oh?" he looked interested.

"And what was the photo of?" Mr Grayling didn't seem to know about the photo.

"It was a photo of a barn."

Just then Stephanie felt a hand on her arm and a familiar body pressed up to her back.

"But it was too dark to see anything else, wasn't it?" Mark said firmly from behind her.

Stephanie looked up at Mark, his face was

serious for a second then he looked down and smiled.

"I need to talk to Stephanie, please excuse us."

Mr Grayling stared at Mark." You went to visit Gordon that day, did he mention the barn?"

Stephanie felt Mark freeze next to her and he turned back.

"Yes, I did go to see him. He answered the door and told me he was fine. No, he didn't know anything and no I didn't go inside."

Mr Grayling looked like he was going to say something but turned away instead. Mark led Stephanie towards the door. When they got into the entrance Stephanie turned towards him.

"What an earth was that?" she glared at him.

"I was helping you, Stephanie."

"You call that helping? Like you care!"

"I do care! You should stop going round showing that photo to everyone."

"I wasn't showing anyone the photo, and I wanted to know what his reaction was going to be!"

"Did you get the reaction you wanted?" His voice was tense, and he sounded tired.

"Well, he didn't go all weird on me like someone I could mention. Why didn't you tell me you went to visit Gordon?"

"I didn't tell you because there wasn't anything to tell. I was shocked when you said he was dead as he was alive when I saw him."

"What time did you speak to him?" Stephanie was trying to piece the timeline together.

"I think it was about 7pm. I was going to visit earlier but I was working late. Like I said, he came to the door. He looked really tired as if he'd been asleep and he told me he was fine and thanked me for coming."

"Did you ask him if Mary had told him anything?"

"Yes. I went so you didn't have to. I was going to tell you when I saw you the next evening, but you told me your news first."

"There seems to be a lot of things you are not telling me Mark."

"If you mean Kate, she left after you went. I directed her to the nearest hotel with a spa."

"So, she's not gone far then!"

Stephanie saw Lisa coming out and saw her chance to escape. She linked arms with her friend, and they left before Mark had a chance to say anymore.

12
A TALK WITH JOHN BARRY

"We could go and talk to John Barry. We could see if he knows about the deaths and show him the photo of the barn."

Stephanie and Lisa were sitting in the classroom at lunch time. Finally, children had stopped coming in and out and they had a chance to talk.

"He probably will deny knowing anything," Lisa said.

"Probably, but I'd like to see if he reacts to the photo."

"So, what's with Mark? Why is he acting so weird about it?" Lisa wondered.

"I'm not sure, I've been thinking about it all night. He's acting as if he knows something we don't, but he won't say what it is. Also, I realised in the middle of the night, that if he went to see Gordon around 7 o'clock, then his car might have been the brown, sporty car Mrs Moore saw."

"Oh, maybe it didn't look as red under the streetlights."

"That's what I thought," Stephanie agreed.

"So, we know that Mark saw him alive at 7. Mrs Moore said he didn't stay long, so he must have died after that."

They both sighed. It could have happened any time in the night.

"What we need are cameras. Do you think any of the houses on that road have cameras?"

"Ooh!" Stephanie squealed, "Let's go for a walk after work. Can you come with me?"

Lisa said she could if she could pick her kids from after school club.

#

They found themselves outside Mary and Gordon's house after school. They decided to start with the first house on the opposite side of the road. They looked for signs of cameras in the windows and looked to see if there was a Ring doorbell. No luck.

"We could go door to door and see if anyone saw anything suspicious?' Stephanie suggested.

"Ok but quickly," Lisa agreed reluctantly.

The first house was an old farmhouse on the

corner. Stephanie knocked on the door and a tall lady opened the door holding a chicken.

"Hello?" she enquired

"Err hello," Stephanie stood back, she didn't like chickens that much. Actually, they freaked her out when they flapped their wings and she thought their toes were thin and crooked like witch's fingers.

"Oh, aren't you the two who found the poor man opposite?"

"Gordon? Yes." Stephanie was surprised she recognised them.

"We were wondering if you saw anything that night, after 7 o'clock?"

She thought about it when suddenly she looked around and behind her a small spaniel ran out of the front room chased by a black cat.

"Just hold this will you."

To her horror, Stephanie suddenly had a chicken stuffed into her arms. She held it away from her face as best she could and started to squeal as it wriggled and tried to flap its wings.

"Help Lisa, take it off me, take it off me. Aaarggh!" Stephanie let go of the chicken as it struggled to escape. It flapped around them frantically while they screamed and ran around in circles. The lady returned to find a crazy sight in front of her house.

She ran up to the frightened creature and soothed it as she picked it up.

"No, I'm sorry I didn't see anything."

She gave them a disapproving look then disappeared back inside leaving Stephanie and Lisa panting outside with feathers in their hair.

"Well that went well," Stephanie breathed, picking off feathers.

The next house was Mrs Moore. They waved to her as she sat at the window and quickly moved on to next door.

An old man opened the door and looked at them suspiciously.

"Why are you two here? It's not going to be me next, is it?'

"What do you mean?" Stephanie enquired.

"Well, they call you the Angel of Death at the Memorial Club." He pointed a shaky finger at Stephanie.

"What? Do they?" Stephanie stood with her mouth open.

Lisa quickly spoke to him, "There's nothing to worry about. She really isn't the Angel of Death honestly. We were just wondering if you saw anything suspicious that night, after 7 pm."

"I did see a man walk past. He had a bald head and it looked like he was coming from the side of that house but I'm not sure."

"Did you tell the police?"

"They didn't ask."

Stephanie and Lisa looked at each other. "Thank you very much. Is there anything else you can tell us about him?'

"He looked big, you know like he was a boxer or something. He had a big head. That's all I know as it was dark. "

Stephanie thanked him.

"I have to go now" Lisa looked at her watch. "That was interesting though, never a dull moment with you. I'll see you tomorrow."

Lisa walked off quickly, and Stephanie headed home.

On her way, Stephanie stopped and looked down the lane. Not much further was John Barry's farm. She had never had the chance to talk to him, now seemed as good a time as any...

#

Stephanie stood in the lane leading up to the Barry farmhouse. The house was surrounded by fields, on her right was a small field with two Highland cows in it munching the grass. They eyed her suspiciously as she nervously walked past. She stopped where the path forked- left led to an outside building that could be an office, and the right path led to the house.

"Let's try this building first." Stephanie said out loud, and she walked up to the door.

After a couple of knocks the door was soon opened by John Barry. He frowned when he saw Stephanie and gruffly asked what she wanted.

Stephanie was the first to speak.

"Hello Mr Barry, I'm sorry to disturb you. I was wondering if you were ok as you were very quiet at the meeting."

"Yes. Terrible news. I heard you were the one to find Mary. I'm sorry that you had to see that. What can I do for you?"

She got out her phone to show him the photo of the barn.

"What do you make of this?"

John stared at the picture for a few moments. There was a flicker of recognition in his eyes before they narrowed.

"What is this?" he sounded annoyed. "I haven't got time for this; I have to get on with my work."

"Do you recognise this barn?"

"Yes of course, It's my barn. Why have you taken a picture of my barn?"

Stephanie was surprised that he admitted it was his.

"Are you sure it's yours?"

"Yes, what's all this about?" he sounded impatient.

"Because Mary sent it to me before she died."

Stephanie looked closely for a reaction, she didn't need to. It was plain that he was shocked; he turned pale.

"I….I don't know why she took that picture." He seemed to be thinking.

"What do you keep in the barn?' Stephanie asked intrigued.

"It's nothing to do with me….I rent it out."

"Who do you rent it out to?" Stephanie finally felt like she was getting closer to solving the mystery. She noticed his face change and become expressionless.

"I don't know who he is. It was just arranged online. I'm sorry I can't help you anymore. I have to go now."

The door closed and Stephanie stood there deflated. What should she do now? She was about to leave when she heard him talking inside. Putting her ear up to the door, she could hear John talking, probably on the phone as there was only his voice.

"I have someone here asking questions about the barn. What are you storing in there? …..I have a right to know, I've had my suspicions for a while." There was a long pause.

"In that case the rent's just gone up. You might not want to tell me, but if the police start asking, it will take double the money to stop me from leading them to you…..Good, you think about it but I'll need an answer by tomorrow.."

The conversation seemed to come to an end, so Stephanie quickly ran around the building and waited. He didn't emerge so she walked quickly down the path.

The front door to the house opened and Mrs Barry was standing there.

"Hello, can I help you?"

Stephanie stopped and walked over to her, quickly thinking of something to say.

"Hello, I'm Stephanie, I'm on the Parish Council and I just had to talk to John about the meeting. Are you going to the service on Sunday?"

"Oh yes of course, come on in for a cup of tea." Mrs Barry said warmly.

Stephanie thanked her and followed her inside. The house was quite old fashioned which suited the farmhouse really. The hallway had a little table with a vase of flowers. The front room had flowery wallpaper and the wall had a couple of dark, wooden bookcases full of books on either side of a fireplace. The front window looked out on to the Highland cattle.

"You have an amazing view from here Mrs Barry." Stephanie noted.

"Please call me Jean. Sit down, I won't be a minute the kettle is on already, I was just making John's mother a cup."

She gestured towards an adjoining room which Stephanie thought was the dining room, but she could now see a foot of a bed.

Stephanie sat down and waited for Jean to return. There was a clock on the mantle which had a soothing tick. She heard her talk quietly to John's mother and then she came in with a small cup.

"John's mother's very ill," she said quietly, "He's taking it hard."

"Oh I'm sorry, I didn't know." Stephanie apologised.

"He doesn't like to talk about it, he's very private. She's going into a home next week. He wouldn't let her go but he's manged to find the money for a nice one and she'll have her own big room with a little private sitting room."

"It must be hard. I've heard that care homes can be expensive." Stephanie suddenly had a thought.

"Is that why John has been buying land to build houses on?"

Jean looked surprised, "I didn't know he'd

shared that with you. Yes he's been investing in land for his mother's treatments. We thought we might have to sell at one time, but John sold some land to a housing contractor and that gave him the idea. He's waiting to see if the planning permission will be accepted, but so many people are fighting it. He didn't really want anyone to know because he feels bad about it."

Stephanie now knew why John had been buying land, not because he was greedy or cunning, but because he needed the money for his mother. Stephanie drank her tea and changed the subject to talk about the cattle and the weather.

"Thank you for the tea." Stephanie stood up to go. "I'll see you on Sunday."

This gave Stephanie a great deal to think about. She now knew which barn was in the photo, but she didn't know who was renting it. John Barry obviously did though and had lied about it. Maybe Stephanie should go for a walk past the barn, she knew where it was. There might be a hole where she could see inside. She was getting hungry though, so she decided she'd had enough excitement for one day.

Tomorrow was Friday, she could go for a walk on Saturday.

13
ENTERTAINING KATE

At last Friday evening arrived. Stephanie flopped onto the settee with a well-deserved glass of red wine. Lisa had persuaded Stephanie to meet her and Martin at the pub for 7, so she had time to make a meal and get changed. She'd already put the oven on and had decided on fish and chips. After watching the news, she enjoyed her tea and got dressed into jeans and a t-shirt.

The weather had turned warmer and had felt like Spring had finally arrived, but of course, as soon as the sun had turned in for the night, the air was crisp as Stephanie walked up to the pub.

Stephanie could see Lisa sitting in the window talking to her husband. She walked in and headed straight for the table. Unfortunately, sitting opposite her friends, were Mark and Kate! Stephanie was gobsmacked to see Kate was still in the village. She stood still and Lisa had to rush over and pull Stephanie over. Mark looked nervous and stood up. "I'll get yours Steph, what would you like?" he asked.

"Erm, a glass of red please," Stephanie replied, unsure what to do.

While Mark was at the bar, Stephanie sat at the round table between Lisa and Kate.

At first there was an awkward silence before Lisa made an attempt to continue the conversation.

"Kate was just telling me that she's staying at Woodland Pines Spa…"

"Oh yes," Kate turned to face Stephanie. "It is a quaint place really, and I was just telling …"

"Lisa." Lisa reminded her.

"Oh, I'm so bad with names. Yes Lisa, that we should all have a pamper there- my treat."

Kate smiled warmly at Stephanie but also looked uncomfortable. She leaned towards Stephanie and held her hands.

"I know my timing was terrible. I didn't mean to spoil things with you and Mark. He is adorable, but he is only a friend. He really likes you Steph."

Kate looked at Stephanie, waiting for her to say something.

Mark appeared and sat by the window. He handed Stephanie her glass and she thanked him.

"You're welcome. We're celebrating, I got that contract by the way."

"Oh Mark," Stephanie put her hand to her mouth. "I'm really happy for you, congratulations."

Everyone raised clinked their glasses together and said, "Cheers."

Mark explained to the others about the new contract for Proctor's farm and his meeting in London.

As the evening went on, Kate sort of grew on Stephanie. She was an odd character, but she seemed genuine and spoke her mind. Stephanie admired that. She watched the body language between Mark and Kate as they all chatted. She could tell that there was a close friendship between them, and she noticed that this time Kate was on her best behaviour. She did call him darling, but she also started saying that to Martin as well. At least she wasn't dangling all over Mark this time.

Stephanie stood up to go over to the bar and Mark went with her.

"So, are you still mad at me?" Mark asked, as they waited to be served.

"I'm sorry, I realise now that I should have stayed. But Kate was all over you, it did look like there was something between you. And your behaviour made you look guilty."

"I know I didn't handle it well. Kate is a good friend, but she can also be hard work. She demands all your attention when she's with you."

"I can see that," Stephanie laughed and looked over to Kate. She could see that she was in full flow talking to Lisa and Martin.

"She's also very attractive," Stephanie admitted.

Mark turned her to him and stared into her eyes.

"You are beautiful! I've missed you." He put his arms around her and they hugged each other.

"Get a room you two!" Jack teased from behind the bar.

"Oh, 2 halves and 2 pints of cider please." Stephanie said quickly.

"Mark, I'm sorry I didn't ask you about your meeting, I know it meant a lot to you."

Mark shrugged his shoulders.

"I know you had a lot on your mind."

When they returned to the table, it seemed that a plan had been decided without her.

Kate told Stephanie, "So Steph, it has been arranged that you, Lisa and I will meet at 10 o'clock tomorrow at the Spa."

Kate looked thrilled, Lisa smiled weakly, and Martin grinned.

"You and I are playing golf," he told Mark.

"Cool,"

Mark nodded and looked at Stephanie with a twinkle in his eyes.

"Right," Stephanie agreed, "sounds like a plan."

At the end of the night, Mark called a taxi for Kate and then the threesome walked down the road. Lisa and Martin lived near the school, so they said goodbye at the corner and Stephanie continued with Mark.

"So how much longer will Kate be with us?" Stephanie asked.

"She goes back on Sunday morning so not much longer. Are you looking forward to going to the spa tomorrow?" he laughed.

"I'm not sure. Should I be worried?"

"No, no. Believe me, she will do her best to pamper you. I'm looking forward to it."

"Yes, but you're playing golf with Martin!"

"It will do you good to have a relaxing swim, a massage, girlie chats…as long as it's not about me,"

Mark did look a bit worried then, and Stephanie couldn't help but tease him about that. Thinking about it, it was a good way to find out a bit more about the wild side of Mark Proctor.

When they got to Stephanie's door, they stopped for her to get out her key.

She turned towards Mark and said, "Would you like to come in for a coffee or night cap?"

Mark smiled, "I hoped you'd say that."

#

The next morning, Stephanie woke up next to Mark. The sun was peeping through the curtains and Stephanie pulled the duvet over her head. They hadn't slept much in the night. She flushed as she remembered what they had been doing and her body tingled with passion for this man next to her. She moved her arm over his chest and lay her face onto his warm body. Stephanie felt him react and turn over towards her.

"Good morning," he murmured smiling, still with his eyes closed.

He pulled her to him and gave her a long kiss on the lips. Things were about to get more interesting when Mark's phone started buzzing.

Eventually he had to look as it didn't stop.

Mark sat up. "It's Kate," he sighed. "It's 9:30 and she's checking that we're not going to be late."

Stephanie looked at Mark. He looked cute

with his eyes tired, his hair dishevelled and stubble on his face.

"Don't look at me like that Steph or we'll never be going." Mark warned her.

He reached for her, but Stephanie quickly rolled over and got out of bed laughing.

"We can't be late for Kate or goodness knows what she might do."

Stephanie walked into the shower and Mark quickly followed her in.

"We'll be quick.." he said.

#

"Right then girls, this is the itinerary." They all sat on the settee in their white robes and slippers. Kate had a leaflet in her hand with the treatments available. She had planned every detail for them, and it was easier just to go along with the flow.

The morning was relaxing and fun. In between massages and facials, they were brought water, prosecco, fruit and snacks. They all got on very well and by the end of the sessions, they were planning a trip to London in the summer.

For lunch, they sat on the balcony of the sport's bar, which overlooked the golf course. Stephanie and Lisa listened to Kate describe her life in London, wondering how she had the energy to live that lifestyle. Stephanie thought Kate was a bit cagey talking about Mark. She talked of crazy parties going on into the morning and sometimes going to work without any sleep. When Stephanie and Lisa asked how they stayed awake, she mentioned drugs helped and laughed. No wonder Mark needed a break Stephanie thought.

They watched Mark and Martin walk over to the bar with their golf bags, and Stephanie felt a thrill to see him.

"Hya girls, have you had fun?" Martin asked as he sat down with a cider.

"You all look beautiful and relaxed," Mark said and he sat next to Stephanie, casually draping his arm around her shoulder.

"Did you get a hole in one?" Lisa asked Martin.

Martin laughed. "Mark got a birdie, but I don't think the RSPB will be very happy about it."

"Oh no!" Kate looked appalled. "You didn't hit a bird did you?"

Mark teased, "It was only a magpie."

"Mark! That's awful!" Kate hit him on the shoulder.

"I was only joking!" Mark pretended that she'd hurt him, then he whispered to Stephanie,

"It really was a duck."

Stephanie nearly spat out her gin and tonic. She wasn't sure whether to believe him or not.

"Well despite the bird culling, I've enjoyed my time with you all. I really hope that you will all come and visit me in the Summer. We can take in a show." Kate announced.

Lisa and Stephanie nodded in excitement.

They ordered a light lunch, attempting to stay healthy. When they'd finished, Mark looked at his watch and realising the time he sat up.

"Oh it's a shame but I have to get back to work."

They all stood up and gave Kate a hug.

"Have a good journey tomorrow and keep in touch," Stephanie said fondly.

"Of course, darling. Cheerio!"

Stephanie got dropped off at home and said goodbye to Mark. They agreed to see each other at the memorial service. Mark said he would be going with his parents, and Stephanie told him her family would be picking her up.

Stephanie got changed into her jeans and looked out across the field at the back of her house. It was so sunny; it seemed a shame to stay inside. She felt energised after the morning at the Spa.

"I know, I'll go for a walk and take a look at

that barn by the river," she said to herself.

First, Stephanie called her mum to discuss meeting up for the service. Apparently, grandma was excited about going and was busy deciding what to wear. Malcolm was moaning because Barbara was making him wear a suit.

Stephanie shook her head smiling as she hung up. She put on her boots and a jacket, grabbed some water, a snack bar and set off.

14
IN THE THICK OF IT

At the end of the lane, you can walk three ways. Left leads to the chicken factory. Follow that road to the right and you reach the river. Walk straight forward along the footpath, is the quick route to the river. Turn right, and you go past Proctor's Farm and Mark's house at the end of the airfield.

Stephanie stood and thought about how to get to the barn.

"I think I'll walk forward, along the footpath, just in case there is any traffic and then I won't be spotted." Stephanie thought, after all she was investigating a mystery.

She walked along through a field and looked around, thinking about whose land she was walking through.

"This field belongs to the Proctors down to the river. Then I will walk left towards the barn." Stephanie planned. "Then I'll be on Barry land."

The path crossed over some little concrete bridges as she walked from field to field over the water filled dykes. The ditches were nearly full of a few nights of rain and bad weather recently.

There were a few hares and rabbits running about. They were tricky to see when they sat still. A rabbit looked just like a brown rock from a distance. Birds were busy flitting about; their chirps and trills filled the air around her.

Stephanie climbed up the embankment and finally reached the river. A long stretch of river ran from left to right as far as the eye could see. It moved ever so slowly; you could tell it was moving by watching the twigs on the surface. Ahead of her was an iron bridge. It seemed to just go to a water treatment place and maybe another farm. Teenagers often jumped off the bridge in the Summer, and a few empty cans lay around in memory of hot summer days and fooling around.

Stephanie followed the path left, along towards a small clump of trees. The small woodland blocked you from walking further along the river, you had to follow the path behind the trees and then it led back to the river on the other side.

As she started to walk round the trees, she stopped. Stephanie could see movement on the other side. In the Summer, you wouldn't be able to see to the other side, but early Spring meant the branches were bare. She quietly carried on walking as near as she dare. Men were talking and walking about. There were about five men in front of the barn, and another three by the river. Stephanie couldn't hear what they were saying. She quickly turned round, walked back to the river and rang Lisa.

"Lisa, it's me," Stephanie whispered, "I'm near the barn and there are some men there."

"What are they doing?" Lisa whispered back.

"I don't know yet, I'm going to go closer," Stephanie replied firmly.

"Wait! What if they're crazy people? What if they're drug lords or kidnappers or something?"

"I doubt it," Stephanie thought about the possibility, "In Hibaldton? I think I'll be ok."

"Keep your phone on so I know you're ok," Lisa ordered.

"Ok." Stephanie answered and then returned to the clump of trees.

Mary must have seen something that night to take that photo, and Stephanie just had to find out what it was.

Stephanie, very carefully, stepped over a rock

and put her foot in between two trees. She had to duck under the branches and walk bent over for a few steps. She decided that if she were seen, she could pretend that she was finding somewhere to go to the toilet. There was an opening in the group of trees. Branches tugged at her coat like hands trying to stop her from moving forward, it was as if the wood didn't want her to go further. She crouched down behind a heavy clump of tangled branches that seemed to have grown around each other. It made a good hide for her to peep through. One of the men started to walk over to Stephanie. He held a phone and wore a long black coat which was open to reveal a cream polo neck jumper and jeans. Stephanie looked behind him to the other men. They had their back to her in deep conversation. What were they doing there? They must have finished in the barn because the door was shut. She looked over to the river, they seemed to be looking up towards Rigby, she couldn't see a boat. One of the men, from the back, reminded her of Mark. She was just thinking that his jacket looked the same when the man near her spoke.

"Right, so you think the drop's going to be next Saturday morning 0100 hours… Yeah…yeah…ok. We'll be here from midnight.

It should take about half an hour to get here from Hull Marina. Yeah…we'll be waiting. "

Stephanie suddenly had pins and needles in her foot. As she shifted her weight from one leg to the other a twig snapped. The man looked up and his eyes scanned the area. Stephanie held her breath for what seemed like ages. She didn't dare move an inch. His hand moved to his waist and Stephanie thought she could see a gun peeking out under his coat.

A gun? People in Hibaldton didn't usually carry guns. Maybe it wasn't a gun, maybe it was a mobile phone. Ok he had a phone in his hand, but he might have two phones….

"Right. No, it's nothing. I thought I heard something but it's probably a rat, there's loads of 'em near the river." With that, he turned back to the barn and they all walked round the side. Stephanie waited, not daring to breathe. She could hear engines starting and then…silence.

Slowly she stood up and looked around to check for rats. The thought of sharing her hiding space with a furry animal sent shivers up her spine. Her legs felt like jelly and were numb from crouching for so long. She didn't have to go back the way she came. Stephanie walked around the thicket and was in front of the barn where the men had been standing. She realised that she was hardly breathing so she took a deep breath.

"What's happening?" she heard Lisa ask on the phone.

"They've gone," Stephanie replied.

"There's a padlock on the barn door, I can't see any windows or gaps in the walls." Stephanie walked around searching for a way to see inside.

"I'm going to come back next Friday night," Stephanie decided.

"Are you crazy? We should call the police."

"They're not going to do anything. We need proof. If I come back, I can hide back there and film what I see."

"It will be so dark, you won't catch a thing."

"Well they probably will have lights, and they'll be talking. They said something was being dropped off at 1 in the morning. What do you think it could be?"

"I don't know but whatever it is, it's worth killing over."

"Maybe it's drugs, or money, or stolen goods."

Stephanie had reached the river again. She stopped and her eyes traced the line of water as it flowed towards Rigby, it's movement caught clumps of green algae and floating branches. It looked dark and deep and cold.

"The river flows through Rigby and then it eventually leads to the Humber doesn't it?"

"Yes," replied Lisa. "My dad's friend has a boat moored in Rigby and he often goes up the river.. You can get to the sea if you want to."

"The man said something about Hull Marina. So whatever it is, it's coming in from the sea. That's how they're doing it.. A ship must bring the goods in, and then they transfer it to a small boat, that brings it here down the river. It's a quiet area, no one around to see. Perfect for smuggling..."

"This is John Barry's land, isn't it?" Lisa asked thoughtfully.

"Yes," Stephanie replied. "I think he recognised the photo and rang somebody up to tell them."

"Do you think he knows what's going on?"

"I think so. I overheard him talking, and it sounded like he was asking for money to keep quiet."

"I really think we should tell someone Stephanie. It sounds dangerous. What about Mark?"

"If I told Mark, he'd stop me from coming. I promise I'll be really careful."

"I wish you'd change your mind. I'm worried something's going to go wrong."

"Look, I know what I'm doing. I'll see you tomorrow but don't say anything in case someone hears." Stephanie hung up.

She felt the adrenaline running through her body. It was up to her to solve this, no one else was going to. She owed it to Mary.

15
IN MEMORY OF MARY AND GORDON

The sun was determined to find a gap in the curtains. The clocks had gone forward on hour, Stephanie carefully opened her eyes to look at the time. It showed 8:30. Well it was really 7:30! Far too early to wake up. However, Stephanie knew that her parents and grandma would be arriving at 9. She willed herself to wake up. Stephanie reached for her phone to see if there were any messages. None. Time for a shower and breakfast.

In the shower, Stephanie thought about the barn by the river. Ok, so this mystery wasn't about selling land to buy houses. It was more daring. Stolen goods or drugs, whatever was in that barn was the answer. John Barry knew who rented the barn. He needed money and even if he didn't know who it was, he could contact them.

If Stephanie could find out what was in the barn, then she could tell the police. But what if the drop off was then taken away? She would have it on video. Yes, she could try to video the van registration plate. Maybe if she waited on the other side of the river? Stephanie got out and dressed in grey trousers and a blouse.

In the kitchen, she emptied a box of Shreddies into a bowl and went to the fridge for the milk. She wondered if there was a place she could hide across the river. But if she were seen, there wouldn't be an easy escape as the bridge was the only way back, unless she walked all the way to Rigby. Her best bet was to hide in the same place she was in before. If she got there early, she could make it more comfortable and check for rats! She hoped that they parked their van by the shed door.

\#

Stephanie watched TV while she waited for her family to arrive. Her parents were going to drop Grandma Bettie at the church and leave their car at Stephanie's house.

A current affairs programme was on, but she wasn't really paying attention to it. Her mind returned to thinking about the mystery. At the church would be John Barry and his wife. She had learnt a lot from talking to her, Stephanie wondered if she would have the opportunity to talk to her alone again.

The front door opened and in walked Barbara and Malcolm. Her dad looked uncomfortable in a suit. They were both retired, but Stephanie's mum worked at the Primary school as a dinner lady.

"Hello, are you ready?" Barbara smiled and gave her a hug.

"I don't know why I'm wearing these shoes when we have to walk all the way to the church," Malcolm grumbled.

"You can't wear your walking shoes with a suit Malcolm," Barbara reasoned.

"It's not far," Stephanie linked arms with her dad and led him outside. "We've got plenty of time, we can walk slowly."

They walked up the road, passing other people on their way to the service.

"The church is going to be packed," Barbara commented, "We should have set off earlier."

"I'm not sitting on an uncomfortable church bench longer than I have to." Malcolm grumbled. Sometimes he seemed to enjoy being grumpy. "Do we have to sit with your mother? I bet she'll probably meet someone she knows and sit with them," he hoped.

"Is her hair still as orange as it was last time?" Stephanie asked her mum.

"It's pale blue now, she had it done yesterday. It looks ok actually."

"She looks like a poodle," Malcolm grimaced.

Stephanie rolled her eyes, sometimes being with her parents was hard work.

They arrived at the church and walked up the path to the doorway. Standing outside, greeting everyone, was Reverend Pierce and Bryan Grayling. Mr Grayling saw them coming and he held out his hand to shake hands with Malcolm.

"You must be Stephanie's parents, thank you for coming today," he shook hands and then reached for Stephanie's hand.

"My dear Stephanie, this all has been a turbulent time for you hasn't it! I hope that this memorial service can give you some closure," he stared at Stephanie as if expecting a response. He looked concerned and Stephanie just nodded feeling uncomfortable. She pulled her hand away to thank the Reverend and then followed her parents into the old, stone church.

The pews were already quite full, and people talked in hushed voices. Stephanie spotted her mum and dad sitting on the left at the back, so she shuffled along the pew and sat down next to her mum.

"We've got a good view from here even though it's at the back." Barbara said looking pleased.

You'd have thought they'd come to see a play, Stephanie thought. She looked around for anyone she knew. She could see Lisa and her family on the right nearer the front. Her daughters were smartly dressed in cute matching blue coats with ribbons in their hair. Pheobie was 7 and Sophia 5, both were huddled together, probably looking at an iPad Stephanie thought.

Mrs Moore was standing at the alter fiddling about with the flower displays and ordering a young girl about. Mr and Mrs Cook sat on the front row, Mrs Cook was wiping her eyes with a tissue. Behind them she spotted John Barry and his wife. They both also looked solemn, just staring ahead waiting for the service to start.

A few rows ahead Stephanie spotted the back of a pale blue head. Grandma. She could hear her voice slightly as she chatted to another lady who looked a similar age. She saw her turn and point in Stephanie's direction and when Bettie saw her, she waved. Stephanie waved back and smiled at the lady who looked very interested in Stephanie, a few others turned round too. One of them looked like the old man she had questioned the other day opposite Mary's house.

Stephanie looked for Mark and his parents, but it didn't look like they'd arrived yet. Some more people sat down next to her; the church was getting full. Then Stephanie felt a hand on her shoulder, behind her sat Mark and his mum. Stephanie just had time to say a quick hello when the service started.

It was a nice service, Stephanie supposed, and everyone said so as they followed each other outside. Stephanie stopped on the path at the side of the church and her parents, Mark and his mum joined her.

"It's lovely to see you all again," Bev smiled at Stephanie and gave her a warm hug. "I'm sorry that we are meeting here, under these terrible circumstances, you all need to come to ours for a meal soon."

"Thank you that would be nice," Barbara replied.

Stephanie's mum looked happily from Stephanie to Mark. "How is Sam? I see he's not here today."

"No, it's not really his thing. I tried to persuade him," Bev apologised.

"Huh." Malcolm grunted. "A shame we hadn't met before, then I could've spent the morning with Sam."

"Do you like fishing?" Mark asked, "I bet dad

would love to invite you to fish with him at his lake."

"Oh yes, he'd love that." Bev agreed.

Stephanie's dad perked up at the invitation. "Yes, I wouldn't mind that. I haven't fished for years though. I'll have to buy some new rods."

"Don't worry about that, we've got spares."

Mark and Stephanie walked a few steps away and left them to talk.

"That really cheered dad up, thanks."

"I'm glad. I bet they'll get on together and maybe I'll join them. Are you interested in fishing?"

Stephanie pulled a face. "I tried it once, but I couldn't get the hook out of its mouth, and it freaked me out."

Mark laughed and pulled her close to him.

"Now then Mark," a man spoke, and Mark greeted him with a handshake. Stephanie noticed John Barry talking to Bryan and saw her chance to find John's wife. She left Mark chatting and mingled between the crowd, eventually finding her sat on the wall.

"Hello it's me, Stephanie." Stephanie smiled at the lady as she sat looking so sad.

At the sound of her voice, she looked up and recognised her straight away. To Stephanie's surprise, she seemed eager to talk to her.

"Stephanie, I've been hoping to talk to you." She looked around as if worried about who saw them. "You know when you came round the other day?"

Stephanie nodded.

"When you spoke to John, did he seem himself?" Her hands were clasped together, and she seemed nervous.

"What's the matter?" Stephanie asked.

"That evening, he came in the house and seemed worried about something. He wouldn't tell me what it was about, then we had a visitor."

She stopped and looked round again.

"Who was it?" Stephanie encouraged her to continue.

"I'd never seen him before. He was a large man, bald and he had a foreign accent. They went out to John's office…"

Stephanie waited for her to continue.

"And when John came back, he was as white as a sheet. He still wouldn't tell me anything, but I could tell he was scared. Oh Stephanie, do you know what it's about?"

Stephanie looked at her and thought carefully what to say.

"Did John say anything at all about it?"

"Just not to worry and not to tell anyone about it, but I had to ask you. Do you know who he was?"

"No, I'm sorry, I don't. "Stephanie touched her arm to comfort her. "I'm sure it will be fine, don't worry."

"Thank you, I'd better go and see if I can find him."

Stephanie watched her walk back into the crowd that was thinning out now as people dispersed. Lisa and her family came walking down the path.

"Hi, are you ok?" Lisa asked with a concerned look.

"Yes fine, hi Martin, hi girls."

Pheobie gave Stephanie a hug as Sophia skipped about.

"Ha-ha I think Sophia's keen to get moving."

"Yeah, we promised them some ice cream after." Martin laughed.

"Come on!" the two girls grabbed their dad's hand and pulled him towards the road.

"Bye," Lisa called as they were dragged away.

Stephanie walked back up the path towards Mark who was looking for her.

"I saw you talking with Mrs Barry, is she ok?" Mark asked.

"I don't think so. You know I …bumped into her the other day. We got talking and did you know that John's mum is really ill?"

Mark seemed surprised, "No I didn't know."

"Apparently John has been buying land in order sell for a profit so he can save up money for his mum. She needs to go into a home, and he wants the best for her. She's been having expensive treatment, but I don't think it's been working."

"My mum and dad haven't said anything about it, I don't think they know."

"His wife's worried about him." Stephanie said.

She looked around but she couldn't see John or his wife.

"We're going now. I told your dad I'd give you a lift home," Mark said.

"I think you're his new best friend right now," Stephanie laughed. "Where's mum?"

"I think she went to look for your grandma," Mark grinned. "Last time I saw her she was being chatted up by an old bloke."

Stephanie turned to see Grandma Bettie and Barbara walking towards them.

"Hello Stephanie, I know I shouldn't say this, but I've had a good time. I've been given a telephone number."

She showed them a folded piece of paper which looked like it was torn from the service programme.

"Arthur's such a gentleman," she went on. "He asked me out and his car is a Mercedes."

"That's handy." Stephanie said as they walked up the road.

Mark had managed to park outside the shop. Their group had reached the car and were waiting for them to catch up.

As they got there, Grandma Betty continued talking about Arthur, "He wasn't keen at first when he found out I was your grandma. I don't know why but he seems a bit scared of you."

"Oh, I don't know." Stephanie didn't like to explain the whole "Angel of Death" thing.

Luckily, Mark had come in a 7-seater, so there was room for everyone. Stephanie was dropped off with her family and they waved goodbye to Mark and Bev. Malcolm suggested that they went for a pub lunch somewhere, which pleased Stephanie as she was starving!

It was later in the evening when she finally got back home and had time to think about her meeting with John's wife. So, who was this large bald man? Was he the man with the big head that was seen near Mary's and Gordon's house that night? Why did he visit John Barry? John had seemed scared. Had he been threatened? It sounded like it. Should Stephanie be worried? She had until Friday night to decide what to do.

She felt guilty about not telling everything to Mark, after all she was mad with him for not telling her what he knew. She doubted he would know anything about this man, and he would only stop her from doing anything. She had to find out what was going on, by herself. It was the only way.

16
THE MYSTERY DEEPENS

Monday had been a busy day. Lisa had worked in a different class to cover a staff illness, so it was Tuesday before the two of them could get together. They met up after school as Pheobie and Sophia were at an after-school club. Pheobie had gone to art club and Sophia was at gymnastics. Stephanie and Lisa walked to the shop to get some chocolate.

"Sophia absolutely loves gymnastics, she wants to join a proper club in Rigby," Lisa told Stephanie.

"Is there a waiting list?"

"Yeah, a huge one! We've put her name down but I don't know how long it will be."

"Maybe you'll be lucky, and some children might break a leg or something."

"Stephanie!" Lisa scolded, laughing.

They reached the shop and went in. Clair was

behind the counter, she worked when Mr and Mrs Cook weren't there. She was in her fifties with short, light brown hair and always loved a good chat. Stephanie and Lisa were deciding which chocolates to choose when Clair remarked, "It was a lovely service on Sunday wasn't it?"

"Yes it was." They agreed.

"Did you know Mary well?" Stephanie enquired.

"Only to speak to when she came into the shop. She was a kind lady." She said sadly.

"She was… We know her, knew her from the Parish Council." Stephanie told her.

"I used to be on the council. I didn't like it though… Bryan Grayling was such a bully. She leaned over the counter to talk quietly, even though there was no one else in the store.

"You know he lives at the Old Vicarage? Well, my friend works at the bank where he has a mortgage. Don't tell anyone I told you, but apparently, he had re-mortgaged his house and was in a lot of debt a few years ago…and now he's just paid it all off."

"The debt?" Lisa asked.

"The whole thing, the debt and the mortgage! Where do you think he got the money from?"

"I don't know, where?" Stephanie and Lisa

were intrigued by this piece of gossip.

Clair shrugged her shoulders. "It sounds dodgy to me. Maybe he won the lottery, maybe fraud."

"Fraud?" Stephanie asked.

"I don't know, that's what people say."

Stephanie paid for their chocolates and left. Further up the street, they turned right without thinking and walked towards the Old Vicarage. They both stopped to watch the workmen who were still building the summerhouse. The driveway swept around a large stone fountain, and water trickled from a statue of a boy weeing into a pool.

"I've never really looked at the fountain before," Stephanie said in surprise.

"Wow, he must have had a lot to drink," Lisa nodded.

They stood and watched the continuous stream, then Stephanie's eyes moved from the statue to the windows of the house. Each window upstairs had a box with pretty Spring flowers in bloom.

"Nice house." Lisa said while chewing her chocolate bar.

"Mmm, expensive though."

"Wouldn't like to clean all those rooms," Lisa said.

Stephanie agreed. A curtain twitched in one of the windows, Stephanie pulled Lisa's arm and they walked on into the Village Hall field. They sat at a picnic bench to finish their snacks and Stephanie opened a bottle of water.

"The person who is involved with the smuggling would be rolling in money…" Stephanie said and took a drink from the bottle.

"What, are you suggesting- it's Bryan?" Lisa laughed.

"Why not?"

"There are a few big houses in the village. There's about three that have just been built and that's not including…" Lisa stopped as if she had decided not to say what she was thinking.

"Mark's house?" Stephanie finished for her. "Yes, I know Mark also has a big house, and I'm not sure where he got his money from either. He has a flat in London too, that must cost a lot of money."

"He has a fancy job though. I bet it pays well."

"Yeah, I bet it does. Plus, his parents own their own land. He did say they needed his help though, and John Barry's wife said they were struggling too." Stephanie's voice trailed off.

"I can't believe Mark has anything to do with it," Lisa said after a short silence.

"No, I can't either. Did you notice Kate hinted that he took drugs in London though?"

"It sounds like they had some wild parties. It's probably common to take drugs there, well everywhere really. Do you remember a few years ago when there was a big fight in the estate, that was supposed to be a drug gang dispute? And that was in this village! There were police all over, even a helicopter."

"I'm sure it just recreational drugs, he doesn't seem addicted. I've not seen any sign of drugs when I've been with him," Stephanie said thinking about Mark.

After some silence, Stephanie remembered her meeting with Mrs Barry.

"I also need to tell you about Sunday. I talked to John Barry's wife outside the church, and she seemed scared. You know that large, man who was seen by Mary's house the night Gordon died? Well, he visited them and threatened John."

Lisa raised her eyebrows. Stephanie admitted, "Ok, someone like him threatened John."

Lisa was shocked. "If he did kill Gordon, did he kill Mary? Was John Barry blackmailing him?"

"I don't know if John knows what he's done."

Stephanie tried to remember the conversation she overheard.

"I think he just knows that he rents his barn and suspects he's up to something illegal. If he knew he'd murdered someone, then surely, he wouldn't be stupid enough to blackmail him would he?"

Stephanie and Lisa looked at each other. The sound of a motor started up behind them, Stephanie turned to see a man pushing a huge grasscutter.

"You'd think the caretaker would have seen him around. Frank was there when I found Mary."

They looked across the field to the Village Hall. Frank was walking along, concentrating on his straight lines.

"We could go ask him," Stephanie said.

Lisa looked at her watch.

"I really must go to pick up my girls. I'm sorry. Just be careful! You know, I think you should just go home and leave it to the police," Lisa warned her friend and left.

Stephanie got up and walked towards Frank. He had stopped to pick something off the ground, and he looked up when he saw Stephanie.

"Now then," he greeted her.

"Hi, looks like a big job," Stephanie pointed to all the grass around them. "You could do with one of those sit on mowers."

"I do have one, but it's broken." Frank grumbled.

"So,"

Stephanie wanted to get to the point before he carried on with his work.

"You know the day when I found Mary?"

Frank's eyes narrowed. "Yeah."

"Did you see anyone suspicious around the hall? Did you let Mary in?"

"No there wasn't anyone suspicious and no, I didn't even know Mary was in the building."

"Why was the building open?"

"I was in there, in my room. I was in and out but didn't see Mary. You're asking a lot of questions."

"I'm just trying to piece things together. So, you didn't see a large bald man?" Stephanie asked.

Frank looked surprised, "No. Look I've got work to do."

"Ok, sorry."

Stephanie walked back to the road. She had always been a bit nervous around Frank even though he spoke to her when she passed him walking his dogs. He looked like he had lived a hard life. He was short with not much hair, maybe he was in his sixties Stephanie decided. She was rather nervous about his dogs too, they were Alsatians and very big. It was probably more to do with the fact that Stephanie wasn't used to dogs. Come to think of it, he did have quite a large head…but he wasn't foreign, and Mrs Barry would have recognised him if he was the man intimidating them.

She stopped again outside Bryan's house and thought about what Clair had said. It did seem strange that he had all that money to pay off his loan and the mortgage. He was also very quick to appear on the scene when Mary had her "accident". Could he have been there to meet Mary? Maybe Mary had contacted him at the same time as she had messaged Stephanie.

Stephanie walked home, her head reeling with ideas, she needed to write it all down.

That evening she spoke to Mark on the phone. It was about 9 o'clock.

"Come over and spend the night." Mark said as soon as she picked up.

"I'd love to but I've got school tomorrow."

"So? You can still go, I won't stop you."

"But I'll be really tired. You know we won't get much sleep."

"I know…that's why I want you to come

over."

Stephanie laughed. "I'll come over Friday night."

"Ok. I suppose I can wait, but it's not easy." Mark sounded disappointed.

It's typical, Stephanie thought, that he rings now when he's going to bed and thinks of her. That thought niggled at her as he spoke that she wasn't really paying attention to what he was saying. Stephanie thought about her conversation with Lisa about Mark. She should be able to talk to him about her worries, shouldn't she? That's what being a boyfriend was all about.

"I was wondering something," Stephanie began, "You told me that you had spoken to a detective about Mary and Gordon, have you heard anything about it?"

Stephanie could hear Mark grow tense. "I can't believe that you're still obsessing about that."

"I'm not obsessing about it. It's the first time I've asked," Stephanie insisted.

Mark sighed, "I know, I'm sorry. It's just that I thought we could put all of it behind us after the memorial service. When we're together, I want to think of happier things and not get stressed."

Stephanie stayed silent.

"Look, I am sure that the police are investigating their deaths and we'll be told when they have finished. They can't really discuss what they're doing can they?" Mark continued, "I've just remembered I can't do Friday. Can we see each other Saturday instead?"

"Yeah …ok. What time?" Stephanie asked.

"How about I pick you up late morning?"

"Sure, that sound good."

"See you then. Bye." Mark said and then hung up.

"Bye." Stephanie said slowly and put her phone down on the settee next to her.

She had to admit that she did spoil the mood when she talked about Mary. Was she becoming obsessed? She sighed, sat back and closed her eyes. When was the last time she'd had a good night's sleep? It probably wasn't normal to be going round the village asking questions and spying on people in the woods. She should try to do as Mark and Lisa said and put it all behind her.

"That's it, Stephanie." She told herself. "Stop being suspicious about everybody and just relax. Mary probably did just fall and hit her head. Her husband most likely overdosed on whiskey and pills."

She got up to get herself a drink of water and decided to go to bed.

"In fact," she continued, checking the front door, "That's more likely than there being a double murder in Hibaldton."

She headed up stairs and went into her bedroom. She didn't bother turning on the light, she walked over to the window to close the curtains. Just as her hand reached up to pull the curtain, she noticed a dark figure standing across the road from her house. Stephanie watched as she slowly pulled the curtains together, and she left a tiny gap to peep through. The person didn't move. He or she just stood there. It looked more like a man, Stephanie thought, by the size and height. He was wearing a black coat with a large hood up and he had his hands in his pockets. Just then, a group of men walked past him and he turned to go with them. Stephanie moved away from the window with relief, he was only waiting for them. She continued to get ready for bed and turned on the TV. After about half an hour, she decided to read a book instead. The only sound she could hear was the radiator cooling down as the heating turned off. Then, there was a rattling noise. It sounded like the side gate being opened. Stephanie listened and then she heard it again. The gate was tricky to open from the front garden as you had to reach over the top to pull the bolt across. It usually got stuck so you had to give it a good wriggle.

Stephanie got out of bed to look outside. First of all, she looked towards the gate. She couldn't see any sign of movement on her drive. Her car was still there. She looked across the street, and to her horror the man was still there. Quickly she closed the curtain again. Her heart was racing. Maybe it wasn't a person, but just a trick of the light.

Stephanie turned the light on and walked onto the landing. Turning all the lights on as she went, she walked downstairs and tested the door again. Still locked. She slowly opened the door to the front room and peered in. Why was it now that she realised, she didn't have her phone or a weapon? She looked around and the nearest thing she could find was an umbrella.

"I have an umbrella!" She shouted as she stepped into the front room.

Damn, she thought, she should have said gun or something!

"And I'm not afraid to use it!"

Her voice didn't sound convinced. She turned on the light and quickly stomped over to the patio doors.

"Yes, is that the police?" Stephanie called into

her hand, "You're right round the corner? That's good."

The doors were still locked, the kitchen seemed normal, the utility room was empty, and the back door was still secure.

Stephanie put the umbrella down on the breakfast bar, her hand trembling. The knife block was next to her, and she instinctively pulled out the biggest knife. She felt braver with a knife in her hand and breathed out slowly.

"There's nothing to worry about. It's just your imagination." She reassured herself.

She left the lights on and climbed the stairs back to bed. Before getting into bed, still clutching the knife, she peeped outside again. There was no one there. What did that mean? Was there someone there before or had she imagined it? If there was someone there….where was he now? It's the kind of thing she said when she saw a spider and then it disappeared.

Stephanie got into bed, put the knife under the covers next to her. She reached for her phone and thought about ringing Mark. She lay there instead, listening for the slightest sound.

#

She must have fallen asleep because the alarm

woke her up. Sitting up, at first Stephanie couldn't work out why she felt so tired, then she felt the knife in her bed and it all came flooding back. She quickly had a shower and got dressed for work. As she was making the bed, she thought about putting the knife back. She paused, her hand over the knife, then she left it. She pulled the covers up to the pillows and straightened the bedding.

17
SEEING THINGS?

Lisa listened to Stephanie as they ate their lunch in the classroom again. Stephanie told Lisa all about seeing a man lurking outside her house, and the noise of the gate being opened.

"So in the morning, did you look to see if the gate was open?" Lisa asked.

"Yes, I pushed the gate, but it was locked. It mustn't have been the sound of the gate after all." Stephanie admitted. She laughed, "You should have seen me, I was shaking all over. I even took a knife to bed with me!"

"You must have been scared to death!" Lisa gasped, "You have been looking tired. It must have been someone just waiting for mates on the way to the pub."

"I suppose so," Stephanie agreed reluctantly.

"All this thinking about Mary and Gordon is really getting to you. Maybe you should see someone, you know, a therapist."

"I'm fine!" Stephanie insisted.

After she had finished her sandwich, she thought about the afternoon lesson. Wednesday was PE day and she'd forgotten to wear her sports kit.

"In the rush this morning, I forgot my PE kit. I could rush home and change. If I'm a bit late, you can take the register can't you?" Stephanie asked Lisa.

She agreed and Stephanie quickly left and got into her car.

It only took her a minute to get home. As she pulled into the drive, the first thing she noticed was her gate was wide open. She was sure it was bolted! Stephanie got out of her car and looked down the side of her house. Nothing was unusual. She shut the gate, reached over to try to lock it but she was too short to reach. Annoyed, she rushed into her house and went out the back door to lock the gate. After a quick look around, she ran upstairs to get changed. By the time she had returned to school, she had convinced herself that she was overreacting again.

It was 5 o'clock before Stephanie finished at school. There were stories to mark, and she wanted to look at them in detail. Driving home, she started to dread being home on her own.

When she got to her road, instead of turning, she drove straight on and found herself heading towards Mark's house. She would feel safer if she stayed at his house, she would just go and see if he was in and then go back to get her things.

As she passed John Barry's farm, she slowed down to look over at the house. She noticed a black 4x4 parked in his drive, it looked familiar, but she couldn't see the registration plate. She pulled to a stop. She was blocking the lane so she pulled over onto the grass and parked next to the wall. Sitting in her car, she could just see over the top of the wall. She wished she had her binoculars in the car with her.

Time went by when finally, the front door opened. Out stepped Sam Proctor followed by Mark. They turned their backs on the road to face the doorway. Stephanie couldn't see who they were talking to, as he was inside the dark house, but she guessed it was John. Sam's arms were waving about and at one point it looked like he was going back in, but Mark pulled him back.

Stephanie was worried, Mark had told her when his dad and John had nearly got into a fight years ago, she hoped it wasn't going to happen again. Mark seemed to persuade his dad to get into the car and then he got into the driver's seat. Stephanie quickly backed into the driveway and drove home before they saw her.

Back at home, she got inside and headed for a glass of wine. Ok, it probably wasn't a good idea on an empty stomach, so she opened the cracker box and went to the fridge for some cheese. She sat at the dining table and started to mark her class's stories. They were good, Stephanie was pleased they were starting to use their imagination. After she had marked half of them, she realised how hungry she was, so she got up to make Spaghetti Bolognese.

Stephanie put on some cheerful music; 90s music was usually her go to for cheering her up. She needed to de-stress and take her mind off everything that was happening. Everyone was right, she was starting to see things that weren't there. She was jumping at the slightest noise and becoming suspicious of people she'd known for years.

As she was throwing the onion skin away, she noticed the bin was full. She took the bag out and walked through the utility room to the back door. She went to turn the internal lock which unlocked the door, but it was already turned. Had she already been out? Puzzled, she carried the rubbish to the bin and returned. This time, she ensured the lock was turned.

By the time tea was ready, she was already in a much better mood. She sat at the table to eat. Spaghetti was her favourite, with flat garlic bread.

"I'd better finish these stories," she said out loud.

Outside was already dark, just the twinkle of lights from her garden lanterns. She didn't have any curtains in the kitchen as there was a field at the back.

After her meal, she moved into the front room with the last of the books and realised she hadn't closed the curtains. She knelt on the settee to pull them across, and something caught her eye across the road. It was hard to see as her lights were on. Curtains drawn, she stood up and took a deep breath. What should she do?

She picked up her phone and checking the front door was locked, she ran upstairs. Without turning on the light she crept up to the window and peeped round the curtain. Yes. Standing opposite, like last night, was a man dressed in black- just staring ahead towards her house.

Stephanie took a photo with her phone. It worked quite well, she could zoom in on the figure, but still couldn't see his face. At least she had proof she wasn't seeing things.

Maybe it was the wine, maybe she was just stubborn, but Stephanie was mad. She stood in front of the window, clearly and calmly she closed the curtains. She wasn't going to be intimidated by anyone! Someone was definitely trying to scare her, and Stephanie wasn't going to show it. Yes, she was absolutely creeped out, but they didn't know that. This only made her sure that she was on to something!

After getting ready for bed, surprisingly it wasn't long before she fell asleep. In a strange way, she felt relieved that she wasn't going crazy.

If she had felt for the knife, that she had left under the covers, she might not have been so brave… as it was no longer there.

#

The snooze alarm woke Stephanie up, eventually. Realising she was late, she didn't bother with a shower. Stephanie just pulled on the clothes she was wearing the day before and headed downstairs. In the kitchen, she grimaced when she saw the dirty plates and pans from the night before. Quickly, she shoved them in the dishwasher and grabbed a banana from the fruit bowl. As she turned, she glanced outside and saw her underwear on the washing line. That was strange because she didn't remember hanging any washing out for ages. How long had that been there? She didn't have time to think about it. She jumped into her car and sped off to school.

All day, Stephanie tried not to think about the menacing man outside her house, she didn't say anything to Lisa about it either. It was better to just get on with the day as if everything was normal.

At the end of the day though, she knew that she had to come up with a plan, she didn't want to be on her own again. Instead of going home, she drove towards Rigby. Stephanie kept checking her mirror, in case anyone was following her, but to her relief the roads were empty.

On the way to her parents' house, she thought about what to say to them. She needed a reason to stay there because she didn't want to worry them. The boiler could be broken! That's it!

Just to be on the safe side, she drove around the estate and then quickly darted into her parent's road. She pulled into their drive and just managed to fit her car behind her dad's.

"Hello," Stephanie called as she let herself in.

"Oh, this is a nice surprise! What are you doing home?" Barbara came out of the front room to greet her.

"My boiler's broken," she moaned, "Can I stay here until its fixed?"

"Your boiler's broken?"

Her dad came out and they all stood in the kitchen. Her mum put the kettle on to make them a cup of tea.

"I'll go round and have a look."

"No, it's ok dad, someone's coming out on Friday," Stephanie opened the cupboard to get out some mugs for the tea. She thought if she didn't look at them, her lie would be more believable.

"Tomorrow! That's rubbish," Malcolm complained. "It probably just needs a service; I can do it tomorrow. Why are you paying someone anyway when you can call me?"

"Please dad. It's ok, and it means I get to spend some time with you. It will be a nice change… and I have a service agreement."

"Yes Malcolm," Barbara smiled, "We can spoil you; you look so tired!"

Her mum put her hands on either side of Stephanie's face and stared at her with a worried look. She put her hand on Stephanie's forehead, like she used to do when she was little. Stephanie laughed and brushed her mum's hand away.

"I just need an early night and need a holiday, that's all."

Stephanie poured out the water while her mum got the milk, then they all sat in the front room to drink it.

"Where's Grandma?"

Stephanie asked looking over at the chair that she usually sat in.

"She's on a date," Barbara smiled.

Malcolm rolled his eyes, but Stephanie's mum told him off.

"She deserves to go out and have some fun. You don't stop wanting to have fun when you get old you know!"

Malcolm sighed and pretended to be busy choosing what to watch on the telly.

"I don't care what she does, but I just don't need to hear about it when she comes home that's all," he mumbled.

Stephanie relaxed and chatted to her parents. It was nice not to have to cook in the middle of the week, and she felt much safer with them than in a house on her own.

Once in her old bedroom, she looked around. Her desk was in front of the window which looked onto the back garden. It was bare apart from a white jewellery box. Stephanie picked it up and felt for the wind-up key at the back, which she gently turned. Next, she opened the lid and smiled as the familiar music started and an entrancing ballerina twirled in front of the tiny mirror. Stephanie replaced it and wandered around the room. Old cuddly bears looked snug together on the bed, a Scooby Doo ornament sat on a shelf next to a model of The Mystery Machine and an abandoned tennis racket stood on the floor next to the door. It was like being transported back in time. Stephanie picked up The Mystery Machine and turned it in her hands. She wished that the Scooby Doo gang could help her solve this mystery. What would they do?

After getting changed for bed, she thought about the approaching Friday night and the stakeout in the woods. She had nearly given up the idea but that man trying to scare her, just made her even more determined to find out what was going on.

In her desk drawer, she got out a notepad and a pen. She doodled at the side as she planned what she'd need to take for her stake out. A flask of tea, a hot water bottle, thick socks and black clothes. She realised that she had become fixated with keeping warm, so she focused on other things. Binoculars, iPhone for recording, snacks and… should she take a weapon? The thought of having a knife made her worry in case she did have to use it. She wasn't great with blood. She remembered she had a heavy torch. A torch! That would be a good idea too.

She went downstairs for a drink. In the darkness of the cool kitchen, she couldn't help peering outside to check if there was anyone loitering about. The dark street was lit by a nearby streetlamp, and Stephanie held her breath as she scanned up and down the road. No one was there.

Back in her room, she checked the back garden too. Feeling satisfied that everything was fine, she returned to doodling in her notebook. It wasn't long before she fell asleep, still holding the pen in her hand.

Something woke Stephanie up. It was dark in the room and for a minute she forgot where she was. Stephanie sat up to listen, she could hear someone slowly creeping up the stairs. Some of the stairs squeaked and a floorboard creaked outside Stephanie's room. The footsteps stopped and Stephanie held her breath. She could hear heavy breathing outside her door and the door handle turned slightly and then stopped. Stephanie couldn't believe how stupid she'd been to put her parents in danger. Without hesitation, she flung herself out of bed, picked up a tennis racket and threw open the door.

"Aarghhh!" Stephanie screamed waving the racket wildly in the air.

"Aaarghhhh!" screamed Grandma Bettie.

"Aaaarghhhh!" screamed an old man nearly falling down the stairs. He clutched his chest and Grandma Bettie grabbed him before he fell.

Barbara and Malcolm appeared on the landing.

"What the hell is going on?" Malcolm shouted.

He looked from Grandma Bettie to the strange man to Stephanie. Stephanie was standing over him, still with a racket over her head, frozen.

"She tried to kill me!" the old man cried and turned to go down the stairs. "It's not my time!" he shouted back.

"Alfred, it's ok she didn't mean it, she sleepwalks!" Grandma Bettie sighed and looked at Stephanie.

"Oh well, you win some you lose some," she shrugged and then went off to bed.

Stephanie looked over to her mum and dad, who were still standing there in shock. Stephanie didn't know how to explain anything that had just happened, so she said, "Night then," and quickly shut the door.

"What just happened?" Malcolm asked his wife, "All the neighbours will think I'm murdering everyone in their beds!"

"Go back to sleep dear," Barbara said, and Stephanie heard her go downstairs to lock the door.

Stephanie lay awake, her heart still beating fast. It was official, she was going crazy and when Arthur got back to Hibaldton, everyone would think so too! Hopefully Arthur wouldn't be keen to gossip about sneaking upstairs with her grandma in the middle of the night.

In the morning, Stephanie felt like she'd been run over by a bus. She smiled as she crept past her grandma's bedroom. It sounded like a bear was sleeping in there she snored so loudly.

Barbara was in the kitchen and had already made a cup of tea and some toast.

"Thanks mum,"

Stephanie kissed her mum on the cheek and quickly glugged down her tea.

"I'll take the toast to go."

"Will we see you tonight?"

"Hopefully my boiler will be mended. I'll let you know."

She shouted bye to her dad, got into her car and drove to school.

18
THE STAKE OUT

All day, Stephanie couldn't stop thinking about the night ahead of her. She'd talked herself out of it three times but she kept reasoning that it had to be done. When home time came, Lisa was standing in the classroom waiting for Stephanie to return.

"What's going on?" Lisa demanded.

She knew her friend too well to not notice she was acting strangely.

"Nothing, why?"

Stephanie tidied up straightening the tables.

"Wow these kids just pretend to put things away. Look he's just left his reading book on the windowsill!"

"Stephanie!"

Lisa walked up to her.

"You have been distracted all week. If there is something wrong, tell me."

Stephanie didn't want to tell her about the return of the creepy stalker, she'd either think she was going crazy, or she would insist that she stayed at her house.

"Oh no!" Lisa remembered. "You're not going back to the barn tonight are you? Are you still doing that?"

She followed Stephanie around the room.

"You are crazy, it's freezing outside. You'll fall in a ditch or get kidnapped!"

By now Lisa was waving her arms about. The door opened and Tracy, the teacher from next door came in. The two of them froze.

"Have you seen the big paper strimmer?" she asked looking from one to the other.

"No. Not seen it." They both said together.

The door closed and Lisa stood in front of Stephanie.

"Look, I can see that you are serious about this, and maybe you need to do this to convince yourself that there is nothing going on. But please make sure you send me a text if there is anything wrong. I'll keep watching my phone. Promise?"

Stephanie promised. She hugged her friend and grabbed her coat.

#

When Stephanie got home, she looked around to make sure her house was safe. The gate was open again. Stephanie was annoyed. She crossed over the road to where the man had stood. There were about 4 cigarette butts on the ground. Evidence! She got a tissue out of her pocket and picked them up.

"Right Mr Stalker, I have a photo and now DNA, let's see what else you leave me. Ha!"

She marched over to her door and let herself in. The first thing she did was put the evidence into a food bag and put it safely in the drawer. She looked outside at the washing line. No panties. She walked over to the patio doors and opened them. Ok so now she knew whoever he was, he had her underwear. She walked about, looking for clues. She was disappointed there wasn't even a footprint. Well, it was grass and patio. She shut the side gate and pushed her wheelie bin up to it. It was full, so it would be harder to open the gate. She needed a padlock.

Once inside she heated up the spaghetti and made sure she had a good meal inside her. As she ate, she thought about what Mark was doing. Why couldn't he see her tonight? Well, it was fortunate anyway that she didn't have to make up an excuse to not see him.

After she'd cleared up, she went upstairs to

get ready.

Reaching up to a high cupboard, she managed to get down her rucksack. She hadn't used it in ages. She put it on her bed and started to look around for things to put in it. Stephanie found black clothes and her ex-boyfriend's kaki green jacket in the wardrobe. Next, she took the bag downstairs to find the rest of the things she'd need.

Soon it was starting to get dark. Stephanie looked at her watch, it was 9 o'clock. She decided she would wait until 10 before setting off. She watched TV to take her mind off it.

"Right, time to go." She told herself. "Don't over think it or you'll change your mind."

Stephanie walked into the kitchen to fill a flask with hot tea, she pulled a black hat over her head and locked the door behind her. There was no stalker waiting for her across the road, she noticed with relief. Stephanie bundled the rucksack in her car and set off.

#

Stephanie tried to get comfortable in the hide. It wasn't too bad. She'd put a blanket on the ground and gathered some branches from nearby to lean over her head. It was quite cosy, and she felt sure that it wasn't noticeable from the barn. There was just a big enough gap to see through and the only problem she could think of was if she needed the toilet. Then because she'd thought of that, she did need the toilet. Damn! She crept out and crouched down near a tree. Animals in the wild peed in the woods, she was sure that this wasn't any different. Stephanie climbed back into her hiding place and waited.

Every now and again, she had to change her position and bend her knees up to her chest. There wasn't a lot of room in there and she kept getting pins and needles in her foot. Her phone said it was 11:32. Stephanie sighed, she probably had got there too early, but she hadn't wanted anyone to see her go in.

Then she heard an engine in the distance, getting closer. It didn't sound like a car... a boat? Stephanie peered through the gap. She could see the barn and the land next to the river, but she couldn't see any sign of movement. She could hear the engine slow down, and then it sounded like the boat continued further down the river. That was strange because it was too dark for a river trip, plus the river didn't go anywhere interesting unless you lived in a village that way. Maybe someone was going home she supposed. Stephanie continued to listen. She thought she could hear a voice in the distance and the noise of cars in the distance, then, nothing.

A while later she could hear another car, but it didn't come near. Stephanie decided to have a hot drink from her flask, and she felt in her rucksack for a chocolate bar. She took her gloves off in order to feel the heat better from the cup. Afterwards, she rubbed her hands together and put her gloves back on. She was beginning to change her mind about doing this. She couldn't feel her bottom or her left foot anymore. She listened carefully and began to crawl out. When it was this quiet, it felt like every twig she leant on made a deafening sound. A flapping noise overhead made her jump. A startled woodpigeon flew from tree to tree. Stephanie slowly got to her feet and shook her leg, she rubbed it. She could feel the blood trickling back down into her foot.

Suddenly, the sound of an engine floating across the damp night air. Stephanie darted back inside the den and huddled up. She found her phone and checked it was still charged up. The noise was coming from the road and was getting near. Finally, there was someone coming. At first Stephanie was pleased, but then she became nervous. She was ok as long as she didn't move, she told herself.

A large, dark van arrived, and parked up next to the barn. Stephanie listened to creaking from movement inside the vehicle. Someone was waiting and not getting out. That meant that there would be more people arriving. She could hear muffled music and smell cigarette smoke in the air. Stephanie waited.

It seemed like a lifetime, then eventually there was the sound of another vehicle approaching. The sound of crunching tyres on the stony path, then the engine stopped. Doors opened and Stephanie could hear voices. Unfortunately, Stephanie couldn't see the registration plates, but she could see inside the van and the car as their doors were left open and the interior lights were on. She took some sneaky photos with her phone, making sure the flash was off. Next, she videoed the men as they opened the barn and their voices could be heard.

"He should be here soon," the first man said.

He had an accent Stephanie wasn't sure, but it sounded Russian. "When boat comes, you two put bags in van. Alex, start loading these bags, now."

Stephanie watched as one man walked over to the river, while the others walked in and out of the barn carrying white sacks and put them into the back of the van. Another man stood by the door of the barn. His back was to Stephanie, but he looked familiar. He had a hat on and a dark coat. He was a silhouette against the light from the shed, but the shape of the hat was like a Fedora, her dad had one that he sometimes wore if he wanted to look cool. The man seemed cold as his shoulders were hunched as he watched the men moving in and out, then he disappeared inside. Stephanie carefully changed position and tried to rub her left leg. She moved her head to try to get a glimpse of the person by the river. He was walking back quickly, and Stephanie could hear the brumming sound of a boat approaching.

The group of men started to move quicker and two of them ran over to the boat as the engine stopped. There were hushed voices and a torch shone in their direction. Stephanie held her phone to video one of the men as he stood clearly in front of her. His face glared at the torch light, and he waved his hand angrily to motion for them to turn it off. Stephanie recognised the man's body shape as being like the creepy man from outside her house! She was sure of it, and she also noticed that his head was bald. He put up his hood and strode over to the boat. She could hear him talking to the boat person, he didn't sound happy, but Stephanie couldn't understand what he was saying because it was in a foreign language.

Stephanie pressed stop on the recording when her phone started to vibrate in her hand. It lit up and Stephanie quickly put it to her ear and pressed answer, it was Lisa.

"Don't ring me," Stephanie whispered.

"Are you ok? I was worried because you haven't rung me," Lisa whispered back.

"I'm ok, I'll text you," Stephanie stopped the call. She decided it would be a good idea to send the videos and pictured to Lisa, just in case she lost her phone. She leant over the phone, and sent it as quickly as she could. She hadn't looked at them, but she hoped that they were clear enough to see.

Suddenly she felt something grab the back of her coat and whatever it was, pulled her roughly out of the den. She dropped the phone and gasped as she fell back on the ground. She looked up to see a surprised face looking down at her.

"Who are you?" A young man asked and pulled her to her feet. "What are you doing?

He looked into the den and reached for her rucksack.

"Move!" he ordered and pushed Stephanie ahead of him and out of the trees up to the barn door.

Stephanie's left leg was numb, and she fell over onto him as they stood at the entrance. She grabbed his jacket to stop herself from falling and they both ended up on the floor.

"Oops sorry," She pushed against him to stand up and the pain in her foot was tremendous.

"Arghh! She shouted, stamping her foot and hopping around.

"What the fuck is going on?"

The bald head man swore in his thick accent and stormed over to where Stephanie was rubbing her leg and stamping it on the ground. She looked up at him defiantly.

"You!" he gasped incredulously.

"Stephanie?"

Another surprised voice came from behind her, and Stephanie swung round. From the light of the barn behind him, Stephanie could make out the face of Bryan Grayling. His face was in shock. Stephanie felt her back being pushed and Bryan stepped aside as the big Russian thug marched Stephanie into the barn.

"Watch her!" he ordered, and the door was shut on both of them. She could hear him shout at a man to stand in front of the door.

"Don't you ever give up?" Bryan Grayling

moaned as he paced up and down in front of her.

"So, it's you who rents this barn! What are you up to?" Stephanie demanded.

"It wasn't supposed to go like this."

Bryan looked nervous, despite the cold he was sweating, and he took out a handkerchief to wipe his brow.

"What's in the sacks?" Stephanie demanded.

She tried to stay calm. She slowly made her way towards the barn door, she thought about making a run for it, but she needed some answers.

"You might as well know, you're not going to be able to tell anyone what you've discovered," he said in a grim tone. "It's cocaine…it's good money Stephanie, I couldn't resist the offer. All I had to do was provide a place for the drugs to be stored and to keep anyone from finding out. The trouble is, I wasn't counting on there being so many busy bodies in this village."

"I thought you cared about this village." Stephanie was seething.

"I do care."

"Right," Stephanie huffed, "You went on about stopping people from building houses, and all you cared about was keeping the village quiet so you could deal drugs unnoticed. What happened to Mary?" Stephanie stared at Bryan and her eyes narrowed. She knew he was an egotist, but she didn't believe he could be a murderer.

"She was on to you, wasn't she? That's why she went for a walk to the river, she was watching you!"

"It…it was an accident," he mumbled. "She somehow found out about the barn. She didn't know it was anything to do with me, but when she sent me the image I had to do something about it. I met her at the village hall, and I persuaded her to go inside. Then…"

He took a deep breath and licked his dry lips.

"We fought over her bag, I just wanted to get her phone so I could delete the photo. She fell and …."

"Hit her head on the table."

Stephanie finished the sentence.

"What about Gordon? Don't tell me that was an accident too."

"Don't look at me like that Stephanie, do you think that I could murder people I have known for years? I had to tell Sergei that Mary might have told her husband. I tried to find out if he knew anything and I didn't believe he did. I told Sergei he was no threat but…"

His voice was shaking by now, he sat down

on a hay bale.

"Sergei told me that he paid him a visit that night. It was him that killed Gordon, not me…I swear."

Stephanie stared at him, wondering whether to believe him or not. He looked pathetic and scared, standing there in the dim light, not at all the commanding presence he usually formed.

He spoke again and sounded panicked.

"Why did you have to come here, you stubborn girl! I tried to persuade you stop asking questions, but no, you just had to stand outside my house, you had to go around showing that photo to everyone…I had to tell Sergei about you!" he paced about like a caged animal.

Suddenly there was shouting outside, someone banged against the barn door. Stephanie opened the door and nearly got pushed as someone ran past. There were bright lights and someone was shouting, "PUT DOWN YOUR WEAPONS! ARMED POLICE."

Stephanie froze, and squinted into the blinding brightness. She was just about to shout for help when John pushed her out of the way and ran towards his car. She fell sideways and was grabbed by a hand that dragged her to the left. At first Stephanie thought it was the police taking her to safety, but the grip on her arm was far too tight. The huge fingers held her in an angry, vice like grip and she found herself suddenly being pulled onto a boat.

Already it was moving away. She didn't even have time to yell. The boat sped away, her arms were held behind her back in a painful squeeze as he stood behind her. Stephanie watched dark figures stare at them as they got further and further away.

19
BRAVE OR STUPID?

The roar of the engine and the gushing of water filled her ears as they tore through the river. In the darkness, Stephanie recognised the bridge in Rigby as they passed underneath at speed. It wasn't until they were again in the open countryside that the boat slowed down a little. Stephanie was crouching in a corner of the boat with the spray of the water around her. She was wet through and freezing, she couldn't feel her hands or her face. At first, she was afraid of falling out into the darkness of the river. Now she was considering jumping in, but the riverbank was so high and full of reeds she wasn't sure if she would be able to climb out.

She looked up the boat and could see Sergei talking to another man inside the cockpit. The boat bounced up and down which sent objects sliding about on the deck. Stephanie reached out to hold onto a bench and pulled herself behind it. She watched as the huge man turned towards her and stepped out onto the deck.

"UP!" Shouted Sergei over the sound of the engine.

He motioned with his hand for her to get up. Stephanie stayed where she was, but when he approached her, she decided it was better to co-operate; for now.

They stood in the cockpit under a blue cover. A man was at the helm, sat in a chair. He was concentrating on the manoeuvres and Stephanie was glad as she didn't want them to crash into the blackness of the night. Drowning wasn't the way she would choose to die, there had to be something she could do!

Sergei stood opposite her with a cruel, thin smile that didn't reach his eyes. His hood was down, and water dripped down the side of his bald head past a tattooed snake that coiled above his left ear. Urgh, Stephanie shivered in disgust.

"Stephanie Rhodes…yes, I know who you are," he spoke in a slow, deep, menacing voice.

He looked her up and down. "I know where you live, I know where you work, and…" he paused and leaned over to whisper in her ear. "I know you have good taste."

Stephanie was not expecting this. He reached into his pocket and dangled a pair of her knickers in front of her eyes. Her eyes must have gone wide because he laughed and put them back in his pocket. Stephanie realised she had given him the reaction he had wanted.

"I'm sure they'll look good on you," Stephanie replied with an icy glare.

She tensed up as he moved closer, his huge body looming over her.

"I like spirit, little girl, but you are not brave-you are stupid," he said staring at her. "At first I am annoyed at you, but … I watch you, I think gods give you to me. My plans are kaput; so I must have something…"

Stephanie stood as still as a statue. She watched him move away to a table and pick up something shiny. He twisted the metal in his fingers, the moonlight reflected off the knife as he held it up for Stephanie to see.

"You recognise your knife?" he teased.

Crap. The full realisation that he had been inside her home, inside her bedroom was now upon her. That was the knife from her bed! Those were her panties! He had got them from her drawer and put them on the washing line to taunt her.

"Well, your plan to scare me didn't work

because I didn't even notice you were there!" Stephanie lied.

She felt behind her back for something she could use. She took off her gloves to feel better. There was something there, it felt like a fire extinguisher.

"Oh, you know. I see you look at me through window. It make me watch you more. It is a shame you stop our game."

Stephanie swallowed and a knot formed in her throat as she realised how crazy this monster was. Her fingers felt around the extinguisher as she tried to work out how it was held on to the wall. It felt like it was a hook, so she lifted it and it moved.

The boat sped up as the river widened, Stephanie watched Sergei and waited for an opportunity. She knew they were getting closer to the sea. She could see the Humber Bridge in the distance and the smell of salty water was now in the air. It was a clear night sky and stars filled the sky. The moon was a small crescent but still shone brightly as there was no light pollution. He was laughing out loud, his open mouth revealed a shiny gold tooth and Stephanie felt like she was going to be sick. He underestimated her, she thought. Sergei stood, relaxed at the table. His hand was lightly holding the knife and the man at the wheel had started to ask him questions in Russian.

"Kuda nam idti?" he shouted over his shoulder.

"Pereyti na korabl," Sergei commanded, and he pointed towards the sea. Stephanie knew this wasn't a good sign.

There was a swell in the river as the tide from the sea swept inland causing the boat to rock suddenly. Sergei stared ahead of the boat and reached his hand out to balance himself. The knife escaped out of his hand and slid off the table into the darkness. Stephanie moved like a coiled spring. She grabbed the extinguisher and brought it down as hard as she could towards Sergei, who was already caught off guard. It hit him on the side of his head and as he fell over, she turned it on its end and thumped him hard in his stomach.

The driver had slowed down as they were approaching another bridge and Stephanie could see boats moored up on the riverbank. Stephanie lunged forward to grab the wheel and she turned it towards the bank. There was a thud as the keel hit mud and the bow scratched against the bank and hit a plank of wood. They fell onto the deck and out of nowhere two figures jumped onto the boat from the dock.

One man jumped on the driver and punched him in the face. The other one threw himself at Sergei and the two dark figures grappled with one another, their bodies leaning dangerously close to the edge of the boat. Stephanie looked around and realised it was Martin kneeling on the other man and was tying a rope around his hands.

Stephanie stared at him for a second, confused as to where he had come from, then it dawned on her that if Martin was there then so was Mark. She turned and stared down the length of the boat into the darkness.

"Mark?" Stephanie shouted and she turned to run along the deck. Sergei had his hands around Mark's neck and was leaning him backwards over the side of the water.

A boat appeared behind them, and a bright search light engulfed them. Stephanie saw the fire extinguisher lying on the deck, so she picked it up and hit him on the back. The blow made him let go and Mark fell to the deck gasping. Sergei's eyes were wild with rage. He tried to grab the metal cylinder from Stephanie's tight grasp, but she held on with all her might. She had hold of the hose with one hand, and the other on the handle. She looked at the pin and with a quick flick of her hand she let go to release it. Thick, white foam gushed out at the man's face as he gaped in shock. It filled his mouth and Stephanie aim it at his eyes which sent him reeling around wildly. His arms were wiping at his face, foam spitting from his mouth, he looked like a wild animal with rabies. Mark stood at Stephanie's side, they watched him topple back and then he fell over the side into the river.

"You fight dirty," he said as he took the extinguisher from Stephanie's grasp and held her close to him.

She wrapped her arms around him and cried, "Oh Mark! Are you ok? How did you know where I was?"

The search light was scanning the water and police were arriving on the bridge. Blue lights were flashing, and people were surrounding them.

Uniformed police helped Mark and Stephanie back onto dry land. Martin was waiting with Lisa and someone came up to them with dry blankets.

"What are you all doing here?" Stephanie cried and she hugged them all.

"I'm so glad you're alright! I was so worried about you," Lisa cried as she held Stephanie's numb hands.

Stephanie looked over at the boat and saw police handcuffing the driver. Others were still searching the river for Sergei.

"I hope we never have to see him again!" Stephanie said.

"I hope he drowns," said Lisa as they walked up the hill to the top of the bridge where her car was parked.

Mark turned Stephanie towards him, "I am so angry with you right now," he said to her, "but all I want to do is take you home and keep you safe."

Stephanie was too cold and exhausted to argue. She got into the back of Lisa's car and the police said they would speak to them in the morning. Mark sat down beside her, Martin and Lisa got into the front.

As Lisa drove home, she told Stephanie how she had been so worried when she couldn't get hold of her. Martin had gone out for a drink with Mark, so she rang them up and told them where Stephanie was. She then ran round to her neighbour to ask her to look after her kids and then drove like a crazy person to the pub.

"When Martin told me, we raced outside, and I was frantic Stephanie! What would have happened if we hadn't have found you?"

"How did you know where I was?" Stephanie

was still confused. She didn't understand where everyone had come from.

"Straight away I rang Detective Jackson. He was already at the barn, and you had just been dragged on to the boat," Mark explained.

Lisa continued, "We drove on to Rigby, but we were just in time to see the boat pass us!"

"So, we carried on to the next place we could think of." Martin joined in. "Lisa drove like a maniac."

"I was going out of my mind. If they took you out to sea, we might never see you again!" Lisa cried.

Mark held her face in his hand and he wiped some foam from her hair. He leaned towards her to kiss her tear-stained cheeks, her eyes and her mouth. She clung on to his shirt and allowed herself to melt against him.

#

Mark left Stephanie to sleep in, she must have been so exhausted. It wasn't until they were sat downstairs, drinking a cup of coffee at the dining table, that they started to talk about what had happened.

"I know why you didn't tell me what you were up to Steph. I've been thinking about it, and I wish I had been more truthful with you,"

Mark began.

"What do you mean?"

"I told you that I had contacted the detective, but I didn't tell you that they suspected it was a drug smuggling operation."

"Did you know Bryan Grayling was the one renting the barn?" Stephanie asked surprised.

"Not at first. When he started asking you questions about Mary, I suspected him. It scared me that you were going around asking questions and I didn't want you to get involved.

"The fact that the police didn't seem to be doing anything was really annoying me. Mary and Gordon deserved more than that!" Stephanie felt like crying, Mark moved next to her and hugged her close.

She continued, "I felt like I was the only one who cared, and that if I didn't do something…"

"I'm so sorry Steph. I didn't handle it right, I thought I was protecting you. You are so stubborn!" he looked at her and laughed. "They definitely didn't stand a chance."

Stephanie laughed too. "Yeah, I guess I am stubborn."

There was a knock on the door and Mark walked over to answer it. In came Detective Jackson and another police officer. They introduced themselves and sat at the table.

"Miss Rhodes, you realise the danger you were in last night, don't you?" Detective Jackson stared seriously at Stephanie. "These are criminal gangs, not schoolboys."

The teacher reference annoyed Stephanie and she tilted her chin up to the detective to meet his gaze.

"I admit that I didn't know the full extent of the situation, but if you had contacted me, I wouldn't have felt the need to take matters into my own hands."

The detective couldn't help being impressed with her bravery. "However, we do have you to thank, as you managed to get a confession out of Bryan Grayling."

"How do you know? Were you listening?" Stephanie was really confused and looked at Mark. Both men looked rather guilty.

"There's something else I haven't filled you in on," Mark said. "Detective Jackson met me at the barn with some of his men last week. We looked around and they planted some listening devices and cameras."

"Was this last Wednesday?" Stephanie began to realise that it was them she saw at the barn the first time she was there.

"Is that when you decided on building a hide amongst the trees?" the detective asked. He reached into his pocket and brought out Stephanie's phone.

"My phone!" Stephanie reached for it, but he drew his hand away.

"I'm sorry but this is now evidence. Great video work by the way."

"Did it come out ok?"

"It was dark, but it will go towards the evidence we have."

"Bryan didn't kill Mary did he?" Mark asked.

"He told me it was an accident, but he knew what would happen when he told Sergei about Gordon. A neighbour of Gordon's told me he saw a large bald man leaving that night, I bet that was Sergei." Stephanie told the detective. "Has Sergei confessed?"

"I have some bad news, Stephanie. We searched the river but there was no sign of him. He could have been washed out to sea we don't know yet."

"What?" Mark stood up. "You mean he could have escaped?"

"Yes, that is a possibility," The detective admitted.

Stephanie shivered, she couldn't believe that this monster might turn up outside her house again. She told them about the nights before when he had watched her house, and how he had somehow got inside. He had taken her knife and her underwear.

The detective told them a knife had been found, and the rest of the gang members were in custody. She had only to call him, and he would send a police car over straight away, even if she wasn't sure.

"Oh, I have some more evidence at home," Stephanie said proudly, "Some cigarette butts that I believe were dropped by Sergei opposite my house."

"That's fantastic," Detective Jackson was impressed. "If you can think of anything else, give me a call."

He left a card on the table, "We'll see ourselves out," he said with a nod and then left.

20
PARTNERSHIPS AND FRIENDS

In the afternoon, Martin and Lisa came round with a bottle of wine. Their daughters were with their granny, so they had all day to chat. They sat in the front room, in front of the fire, and discussed everything that had happened. It wasn't that cold, but Lisa had insisted on the full "fireplace experience" and Mark gave them a tour of the house.

"Wait until you see the house at night," Stephanie told Lisa, "This house is so magical."

"I don't think we'll be around that late," Lisa laughed and whispered, "I have a feeling Mark will want you to himself. Anyway, Martin and I have plans...you know."

Martin and Mark were in the kitchen getting cheese and crackers ready. They came over to the settee and put some plates down on the coffee table.

"So, what will happen to John Barry?" Lisa asked.

"We went round to see him a few days ago," Mark told them. "Stephanie, after you told me about his mother being so ill, I talked to my parents, and we arranged to go over to see them. He had co-operated with the police about the barn. He hadn't known the details, but he admitted that he started to get suspicious when you started to ask questions."

"I heard him asking for more money for the rent, to keep quiet," Stephanie said.

"I don't know if he told the police that, but he told them that Bryan Grayling was renting the barn and he gave them a key to the lock. They had a search warrant anyway."

"I admit that I saw you at his house. I was worried that you were arguing with him."

Mark looked surprised then thought about it. He continued,

"Was it outside? I bet that was my mum talking to Mrs Barry in the hallway. My dad was trying to get her to leave, so I persuaded him to wait in the car. It's thanks to you that we've made peace."

"Really?"

Stephanie felt relieved. Since she had met Mrs Barry, she felt really sorry for them.

Mark continued, "Apparently, they've been looking after his mum for years and paying for private health care. I can see now why he was always in a bad mood and short of money. I told him about the deal I've made with a big company to buy our grain and he's on board too. So, we're partners again, for real this time I hope."

"Let's drink to partnerships and friends," Lisa said raising her glass.

"Cheers," Stephanie grinned, and they all touched glasses.

Stephanie looked around at her friends and thought how brave they were to come and rescue her.

"I can't remember if I thanked you all for saving me," Stephanie said quietly.

"I think you were handling yourself pretty well on your own," Martin laughed. "I wouldn't want to get on the wrong side of you!"

"We were on the bridge, thinking how we were going to get to you, and suddenly there you were crashing the boat into the bank." Mark remembered.

"It's a good job you did," Lisa interrupted, "cos if you hadn't Mark was going to jump off the bridge James Bond style!"

Stephanie's eyes grew wide with horror. "You

weren't, were you?"

She realised how it could have ended so differently. "I am sorry, I…I was stupid to even attempt to get involved with criminals. I won't be doing it again…I don't think."

"What do you mean you don't think!" They all chimed.

"Well…if Lisa hadn't have rung me, I would have stayed hidden. I would have stayed until they had gone and then rung the police, the plan was sound."

Lisa got up to pretend to give her a shake. Martin made a show of pulling her off.

They continued to discuss what may or may not have happened, until Lisa and Martin decided it was time to go home.

As the fire started to die down, Mark stood up and reached for Stephanie's hand. He led her upstairs and into his bedroom. He started to kiss her, tenderly at first, but when he felt her respond to his touch his kisses became more urgent.

As he undressed her, he kissed her down her neck, her shoulders and down her arms. His lips could feel the hairs on her skin react. She undressed him and her hands explored his toned physique, she lay on top of him and their bodies melted into one. He let her move up and down his body and take control, he was mesmerised at her beauty. Her face was glowing, cheeks slightly flushed, her eyes closed and her lips slightly parted breathing faster and faster. He reached to kiss her breasts and let his teeth gently nip her nipples. She sat astride and he entered inside her. Their movements became one, their souls connected and wrapped around each other until they found ecstasy, their bodies reacted feeling the sensation build up and explode around them. Slowly, the rapture subsided leaving a blissful paradise and they lay together in each other's arms, waiting for their breathing to become normal again. Life would never be normal again, Stephanie thought as she listened to Mark's heartbeat. She wished this feeling could stay forever, the two of them in this dream like state.

Mark stroked her hair, and he could feel Stephanie's warm breath on his chest. He closed his eyes and realised that he had never been so happy with a woman. She was his soul mate, she always had been, ever since he saw her on the playing field that day.

"Stephanie?" Mark said gently.

"Mmm," Stephanie was falling asleep and had snuggled down against him.

"We were meant for each other," he

whispered.

#

"Good morning sleepy head," Mark gently woke Stephanie and she sat up to find he had brought a tray with breakfast.

"A cup of tea, orange juice and toast with jam? My favourite," Stephanie laughed and sat up. They ate breakfast in bed and lay together all morning.

"Do you think life is going to be the same now?" Stephanie asked.

"What do you mean?" Mark asked puzzled.

"Well," Stephanie sat up and looked at Mark, "Do you think you'll be staying in Hibaldton now or will you go back to London?"

"That's a good question," Mark replied. "I don't know what the future will bring…"

He watched Stephanie's face and he could see that she was looking upset. "But," he quickly explained, "wherever I am, I want you to be with me."

"Really?" Stephanie smiled.

"Of course! I've been telling you that since I met you. Every part of my being has been shouting this out. Do you believe me now?" he laughed.

"Yes." She kissed him on the lips. Then she

looked worried again. "Do you think Sergei will come back?"

"Don't worry Steph, he hopefully drowned, but I'd be happier if you stayed here with me. We'll go get your things this afternoon. OK?"

Stephanie felt better. She really didn't want to go back home on her own just yet. She thought it would take a while to feel like normal again. It had finally started to sink in that the mystery was solved. Mary and Gordon's lives were taken by those horrible men, over what? Power, money and greed? They got what was coming to them, she hoped.

"Come here Buttercup," Mark grinned.

"Buttercup?" Stephanie wrinkled her nose at him.

"Just trying it out, don't you like that?

"It's ok as long as I can call you, Honey Bear."

He thought for a while, "Steph it is then."

Stephanie laughed.

"Come here," he whispered into her ear…

THE END

Stephanie's adventures continue in the next
book- "Summer Madness."

ACKNOWLEDGEMENTS

Thank you to my husband, Alan, for his enthusiasm and skill formatting my work to be published. To Natalie, my daughter, for transforming my shaky sketch of a book cover into a work of art, despite being busy at university.

Thank you also to Janice, for help with proof-reading the story. Thank you to Ruby and Louise who have given me such positive feedback and lastly, my children Emily and Matthew for their encouragement.

I wouldn't have had the courage to do this without all your support.

ABOUT THE AUTHOR

J L Robinson lives in a small English village, with her husband, a bearded dragon, and a cat that doesn't actually live there but thinks it does. Their three grown children have all flown the nest on adventures of their own.
After teaching in Primary Education for 27 years, she decided to become a supply teacher and is enjoying the variety each day brings.
During this change of lifestyle, her love of reading has transformed into a love of writing.

Printed in Great Britain
by Amazon

11323329R00142